Saint Vicky

Chester Betty

For Amanda
Keep making noise

VICKY VICTORIA

ST. KELL

STRINGS

ACKNOWLEDGMENTS

Many thanks to my betas: Jack, Christy, Shalini and Hamad, who could see things from another angle. Much appreciation to Strasbourg Writer's Stammtisch, who cured me of 36 years of writer's block. And, of course, thank you to my family for their support through all my endeavors.

I.

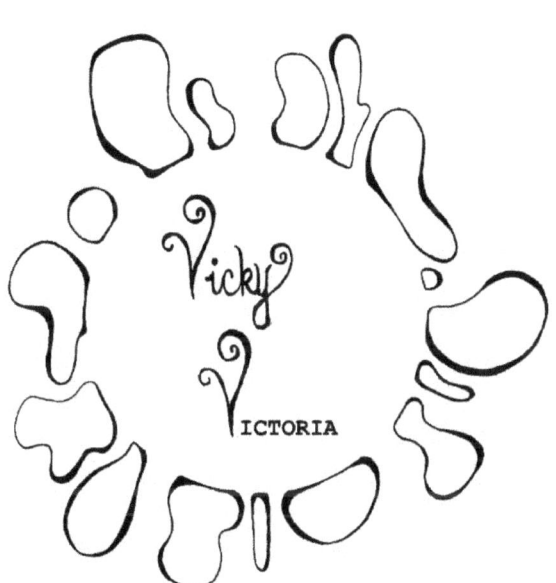

(1980)

Mr. Enders had lived a semi-satisfied life with a charmingly aloof wife and twin daughters until the gnawing desire to liberate his brain from his cranium overcame him. He felt trapped in his body, worse yet, trapped in his head, his two eye sockets providing only a glimpse of relief from the pressure in his skull. He took to sleeping in odd places, moving his bed from room to room until he finally went to the back yard and fell asleep sadly gazing at the shifting stars.

This was the beginning of the end for Mr. Enders, but the end of the beginning for the twins. The four year-olds' mother was tragically lost in a ball pit and somewhere downtown a hand scrawled in Mr. Enders' file, "single father, undiagnosed mental illness." Victoria and Laney weren't talking much before their mother's disappearance, and this did not improve their condition.

Mr. Enders mourned the loss of his analog daughters as their speech became ones and zeroes to his throbbing ears. The pressure in his cranium built until three cars came: one for dear dad, one for each of the girls. Several throats on site were sore from holding back tears as Laney's voice came muffled from one of the cars, "Vicky, Vicky, Vicky…"

MR. & MRS. VICKIE
(2003)

Mike Vickie was no stranger to loneliness—his parents preferred virtually anything to child rearing—so he'd learned to do everything in his power to avoid appearing needy. Sometimes he'd even point at you as he winked; Mike Vickie was a self-made man.

Tricky Vickie had been the only boy on the gym team that could do the human flag, gripping a vertical pole and holding his body horizontally. The core body strength he'd gained, together with a few weeks of practice after his bartending shifts in college, had helped him achieve the degree of apparent spontaneity that he now mastered as he planted his left hand on the bar and swung his legs over the top. He resisted the temptation to point his toes.

*

When he met Vicky Enders, a grown-up orphan who he readily leapt over the bar to greet, he knew he'd met his match. That Vicky had never been adopted, never found the love of a family, didn't stop her confident stride from falling in line with his. Vicky's back story would even help him someday on the campaign trail. Her mother had drowned and her father had offed himself a few weeks later. Tricky Vickie appreciated their hands-off parenting. Vicky was unabashedly happy, down to her contented core, and had no understanding of people who couldn't see all the glory in the world around her. Over the course of two weeks, Mike and Vicky fell passionately in love with themselves. The Vickies were team players.

From the first flirty snowball fight with Tricky's frat brothers, the couple became hooked on public displays of manic love. Following a jumbotron proposal with a diamond just big enough to show up on the stadium screen, but modest enough to show he was One of the People, Mike Vickie abruptly considered himself an adult and hired an image consultant named Jall who was also known as the make-up artist for the "Celebrities without Make-up" series of coffee table books. Jall forcibly removed the "Tricky" from Mike's name and weighed in on his fiancée's identity situation as well. Vicky Vickie was out of the question, so the long version was dusted off and applied. She had never gone by Victoria and was thankful for Jall's help in this first of many ways.

The oversized Vickie wedding portrait, displaying the exuberant couple that had jumped into a pool in a spur-of-the-moment fit of euphoria was a testament to their shared values. The beaming, dripping bride and her joyful husband could be found in several brushed silver frames throughout the tidy home. Victoria had researched waterproof mascara while Mike rehearsed flicking droplets out of his hair. They concurred on Jall's suggestion that Mike do one swift crank of his head to the left after breaking through the water's surface in his tuxedo. This was deemed more "expensive cologne model" and less "golden retriever" than a double crank. The photographer was positioned to capture the moment for eternity. The wedding guests would all recount the tale of the impetuous couple to a minimum of three people each.

*

The newlyweds sailed seamlessly from their honeymoon to Mike's Senate campaign. Jall implored Victoria to mention her past as an orphan at least once a week. "I'd also like to give you a more elegant look, one I call Natural Beauty," he said with an assuring smile. Victoria could almost hear the trademark symbol flitting out of Jall's mouth and hanging in the air.

"First, we're ditching that waterproof mascara-it's too dark for you. I'm adding some length and lightening up on the color." At first apprehensive about fake eyelashes, Victoria learned to enjoy the heavy feeling when she fluttered her lids. The lashes, which Jall assured her were all-natural human hair, provided a shelter for Victoria that accompanied her wherever she went. She felt like she was forever living under two little awnings and took comfort in the tiny shadows.

Jall was full of surprises for Victoria. He delighted her one day with the promise of some sunshine. An hour later she was standing up in a booth, surrounded by spray jets. *Finally,* she thought, *all those foster parents and not one ever brought me to a carwash.* She reveled in the mechanical process and adjusted her tiny fuchsia goggles as the first of weekly tans was sprayed on.

One day Jall showed up with a flat-iron and a box of chocolates. He playfully batted away Victoria's hands when she reached for a molded bite. "They're for smelling, dear! Not eating!" When she could no longer resist, he offered, "Pretend they're little candles. You don't need bigger arms, hon." He proceeded to straighten her hair only to place it in curlers.

"Why are we straightening before curling?"

"Natural wave can't have frizz. It needs to be flat before it's curled."

But the flattened, waved hair didn't pass the bounce test–more needed to be done.

Hair extensions were woven in just like the eyelashes, but then to Victoria's chagrin, cut to match the length of her current hair. "We're going for health, not length. Think robust, Victoria. Robust!" came Jall's wisdom. Mrs. Vickie was thrilled to be able to gather her mass of other people's locks into a fantastic giant bun and didn't dare question Jall's sensibilities when he offered another suggestion: "Cleavage is quite passé. I'd go for a more organic look–I'm thinking saline. Possibly silicone, but we don't want to limit movement."

Victoria reminisced for exactly 20 seconds about all the orphan girls who had chanted "Vicky" as she'd transformed her government-issue cotton bra into what she called her 'tit shelf', a homemade push-up that defied gravity while making interesting leaps in materials science. The brassiere had probably played a significant role in her emancipation from the orphanage and was proudly worn for 2 full years. Unfortunately, Vicky's sexy hoisting system had been made almost entirely of duct tape and other, lesser, bras. Victoria briefly pictured all of her hapless orphan friends who had donated their cotton to the cause, their unsupported breasts swinging around as they swept floors. She nodded approvingly at Jall.

Apparently a near-death experience after a bad reaction to anesthesia will make some people see a bright tunnel. But Victoria swore she remembered taking off from a helicopter launchpad marked "B" and flying silently, effortlessly, to the helicopter's final resting place adorned with a "D". In any case, she woke up two cup sizes more qualified for the campaign trail and with a full body rash. No one told her how many machines had been beeping that afternoon or how long her heart had stopped beating. But when she fluttered open her overburdened eyelids, Mike, in a burst of modern-day chivalry, requested that Victoria modify the Natural Beauty package and keep her nose.

In response, Jall unfurled a fold-out case displaying tools that belonged in the gray zone between art and medicine. "We'll just play around with the shadowing then. Keep the structure, but tone it down a bit." He winked at Victoria and picked up a blending sponge.

*

(2004)

If symbolic cymbals crashed when the couple marched along the campaign trail, no one mentioned it; they just wistfully gazed at the confident pair as they changed everyone's lives by walking by. Victoria's scarves, knotted in interesting ways, were like Mike's smile: you never saw the same one twice. Mike and Victoria Vickie were tangled up at the arm, flashing capped teeth and flanked by security, when they came across a mass of photographers. One stood in the middle of the crowd with her head cocked to the side, her camera lying dormant in her hand. She wore an awkward squint, her eyes scrubbing the couple for a trace of recognition. The photographer was shorter than Victoria and had ruddy skin. She clearly didn't pluck her eyebrows out and then etch them back in like Victoria did, but otherwise it was like looking through a trick mirror: the woman had the same face.

Victoria reached out to her substandard replica with a hand that was expertly manicured with nude polish. "Victoria Vickie. Do I know you? Have we met somewhere?" she said to what could easily be her own self, only pinker.

"Vicky Victoria, and no. No, I think I'd remember you."

Victoria was due for a bronzing with Jall and had penciled in lipstick trials for the afternoon. Jall swore he had found the exact color of her lips and wanted to make sure it looked even under three types of lighting. She decided to invite the photographer to coffee instead.

That afternoon, Vicky and Victoria tried. They tried to remember. They tried to understand. They even tried to sit at the same table for one whole hour together as the pink one told the gold one they must be sisters, that they'd been missing each other all these years, hadn't they? But Victoria shook her head slowly. No, she couldn't miss someone she didn't know. She couldn't love someone she'd never missed. She'd grown up alone. Not sad, but alone. And that wouldn't change when she looked across the table at her other self. The reunited pair hugged for one uncomfortable minute, fifty-nine seconds longer than either would have preferred, and parted ways again, each hoping the other would let go again for good.

*

Like most summer evenings, Mike walked by in Superman underpants on the way to the shower, without resisting the temptation to snap Victoria with a towel along the way. "Ouch," Victoria started, but she felt a sense of acceptance in Mike's incessant needling. She remembered the glow she felt the first time Mike had lovingly rubbed mashed potatoes into her bangs and now fully sponsored a toothy grin as he stepped into the spray. As the water tinkled, Mike threw his red underwear so that it resembled a super hero cape, cresting in her bedroom until it fell on the floor, the 'S' logo face up. That instant, something changed in Victoria and she remembered.

Laney. Laney with her rainbow pillowcase and unicorn pajamas. Laney with her wet hair pressed against her cheeks, her eyelashes clumped into points like the Statue of Liberty's crown. Laney. Her teeth were so small. She was singing, now laughing, now singing.

> Superman, Superman, never give up.
> Superman, Superman, you can see the flowers grow.

Victoria chimed in as she had in the mildewed shower of her childhood.

> Superman, Superman, fly up to the sky!

It was a shower song obviously composed by and for four year-old twins. With a thrilling sense of urgency, Victoria rifled through her wallet for the photographer's card; she'd held on to it for a year now. The photographer picked up almost immediately.

"Vicky Victoria? You're Laney. You're my sister, Laney."

The photographer laughed with relief, like she'd known all along what Victoria had allowed herself to forget. "Vicky," she said, "we're going to a funeral. Have you ever been on a hot air balloon ride?"

CARL
(2004)

The medical file on Carl Enders detailed the ambulance workers' efforts to save him after he had been found by his tot daughter with a power drill in his left hand and a Jackson Pollack smattering of different layers of cranium on the bathroom mirror. Once evaluated and transferred to Saint Tabitha's, a hybrid of homeless shelter and psych ward intended for veterans, Mr. Enders was for all practical purposes dead for the next 24 years.

Carl's resurrection came in the form of Viswanatha Suresh Venkataraman, a doctor on a study visit who was affectionately called Dr. Vicky by the St. Tabitha staff. Dr. Vicky smiled broadly and spoke in a sing-song accent anchored during his adolescence in Mumbai. He had come to the underfunded facility to meet 14 long-term patients who had earned the unfortunate label of being dangerous to self or others, thus guaranteeing that their lazy shuffle between bed and TV would continue ad infinitum.

Dr. Vicky had been examining the files on this archaic set of patients that continued to be "kept safe" in the sense of a more ignorant time. They were medicated with a delicate balance that allowed them to feed and relieve themselves, but which rendered their bodies and minds too heavy to be useful for much else. One such patient, Carl Enders, had been checked in 24 years prior and had been sentenced to the dragging feet and yellow-cast light of his present condition shortly after arriving at St. Tabitha's.

The notes from the team evaluation on Mr. Enders one week after his arrival attested to a violent detachment from reality. He'd screamed and told the doctors they didn't exist. He'd removed his head bandage and tried

11

to rip out his stitches. When all was over, a social worker had a black eye and Mr. Enders had a black mark on his file. The 15 minutes of fame before the St. Tabitha panel had cost him a quarter of a century.

The team that had evaluated Mr. Enders consisted of two doctors, two nurses and the aforementioned social worker, Victoire Lambert. None had been at St. Tabitha's in over 15 years and their orders had never been reexamined, which explained Carl's perpetual yellow haze. Dr. Vicky wanted to know more about the patient with the twinkling grey eyes and injured cranium. He ordered an incremental reduction of Carl's medication over a 15 day period and came to observe him every afternoon.

On the seventh day, Carl's feet picked up and took actual steps rather than keeping constant contact with the floor. By the tenth day, he looked at Dr. Vicky when he entered the observation room, letting his eyes follow the tall, thick man as he wrote in his notebook or bent to tie his shoe. On the thirteenth day, he stretched his hand out and said, "Carl Enders," as he looked over Dr. Vicky's shoulder.

Dr. Vicky beamed and put his huge brown hand around Carl's little bony one, giving it an enthusiastic shake. "It's so nice to finally meet you. I'm Dr. Vicky."

"I had a daughter named Vicky in another life. I called her Superman," said Carl as he made an effort to bore his stare in the vicinity of the doctor's dark eyes.

"Could she fly?"

Carl smiled. He was still holding the doctor's hand and now placed the other on top of it, making sure he couldn't let go. "It was a Nietzsche reference. Is your name really Vicky?"

"Well, some people have a hard time with Dr. Venkataraman and Vicky reminds me of someone dear to me as a child so-"

"Venaktrama, Venaktarama," stumbled Carl. He had so wanted to prove himself superior, but failed where others had failed.

"You may call me Suresh if you prefer," offered Dr. Vicky. "It's all the same to me."

"Suresh. Would you like your hand back now, Suresh?"

"No, you may keep it a bit longer," said the doctor with the same kind smile he'd given an emptier Carl for the last two weeks. Mr. Enders was teaching him things through his desperate grip that Dr. Vicky couldn't hope to learn through routine medical observations. In a few mere minutes with the newly resurfaced Carl Enders, he had felt the electricity retake Carl's brain and body. He could feel the circuit extending to himself as he held on to his hands for dear life.

Moments later, a nurse came through the door and nudged the pair apart. "Mr. Enders has dinner now, Doctor," she said as she took a feeble arm and led him down the hallway that he had always assumed was yellow. *I could be marching to heaven*, thought Carl, *I've never seen walls so white.*

DR. VICKY
(2004)

Dr. Vicky was experiencing the increased heart rate and reduction in appetite that had only ever accompanied the first stages of love. What he felt for Carl Enders could not be romantic, but then to what could he pin this all-encompassing feeling? He was fascinated by Carl, by his description of the world around him, by his understanding of what was happening at all levels of existence. He was surprised to find out that Carl was also a doctor of sorts, who had earned a PhD in theoretical physics in his former life, and started to amicably refer to him as Dr. Enders.

"Suresh, you can read the paper I wrote about simulations if you're that interested," Carl would say when the doctor started asking too many questions.

"Dr. Enders, I'm not sure I'd follow your logic," returned Dr. Vicky. It felt suspiciously like flirting, but their eyes never met. Furthermore, it wasn't true. Suresh followed everything Carl said like it was the pure truth, the center of all that religion didn't have words to explain. He often wondered if what Carl said was the parable or who was saying it. Dr. Vicky was afraid to find out.

Two months after checking Carl out of St. Tabitha's on what was supposed to be a weekend pass, hot drinks now warmed their hands in Dr. Vicky's living room, where Carl had stayed ever since. They drank Turkish coffee while they covered the necessary neurology topics and why Carl had drilled the hole. They drank Rooibos tea as they talked about age-old rituals to free the mind of evil spirits, rituals which were documented in the form of smooth-edged holes in skull remains found around the world. They sipped chili-infused hot chocolate as they pondered the medical understanding of

15

the ancients and whether they had feared that their demons would kill them as Carl had feared the pressure would.

On a tangent from Carl's rambling details about a certain Canadian hot drink, Dr. Vicky learned that the wife who had abandoned him, Claire, was also the muse who had left with just as few qualms. Her tendency to misplace steaming cups of coffee in the morning drove Carl to question whether the mugs were being whisked away to parallel universes, just out of view. Each time he found one in an armoire or a cupboard, cold and filled with lesser parts coffee than brandy, he smiled and told Claire her cup had returned from its interstellar quest. And when she'd floated out of his life, he'd told himself that Claire had simply slipped through the ball pit, into another dimension with her coffee cup, the day she never returned.

Male pattern baldness now exposed a perfect circle set high back on Carl's forehead where the skull was missing and only a layer of skin remained between the soft pulsing of his consciousness and the outside world. Dr. Vicky had to continually hold back the desire to drop his mug and touch the soft spot that served as a reclaimed fontanel. Dr. Vicky came to understand that Carl's crude effort to reinstate blood flow to the full brain, an exercise that Carl believed to be completely independent of his simulation research, had gotten him sent to St. Tabitha's in the first place. Carl's belief that his universe was an illusion was almost irrelevant to his commitment.

Carl's postdoc work on simulated universes had overlapped with philosophy to such a degree that few colleagues has taken him seriously in the 1970s. But he'd co-authored a paper (and perhaps a prenup, according to Dr. Vicky's notes) with someone named Marka Swandish, another physicist who was finally gaining credibility in her field with studies that searched for evidence of an underlying lattice to the universe.

Dr. Vicky was afraid to reach out to Carl's former colleague for several reasons. But mostly he feared that seeing Marka Swandish again would rekindle the intellectual stimulation that Carl had thrived on before the pressure built. Dr. Vicky didn't want to share his new friend with Ms. Swandish, but he knew he'd need to come to terms with Carl's past soon. It was the right thing to do for this man who spoke poetry in his sleep and had two missing children.

He'd researched every possible source pertaining to the separation of the Enders family at both the county and state level. One name had wormed its way into several documents from different agencies: Victoire Lambert. Her business card was paperclipped to Carl's file:

Victoire Lambert
Family Liaison Officer, Level IV

Quatslak County Department of Health and Human Services

VICTOIRE
(2004)

There's not even a phone number mused Dr. Vicky as he turned the useless card over in his hands. To reach Victoire Lambert, he phoned no fewer than six similarly-named tentacles of the family services department only to find that she was retired and living back in Quebec.

Victoire Lambert had nudged the fate of the Enders family more than once. Claire Enders had only prepared one name for a boy and one for a girl, but when faced with unexpected female twins she sat joylessly with her armful of babies and looked out the window to a grey parking lot for inspiration. Two days had passed between her delivery and the visit from Victoire the social worker, a stern French Canadian who had been sent to deal with Claire's acute postpartum depression. Victoire's efforts to convince the couple that two babies were indeed better than one were heavily responsible for the naming of baby number two on day number three. "Victoire" wasn't quite American enough for Carl, but they were both happy to call her Victoria so that she could share a nickname with the visiting County Health Board angel.

Victoire Lambert stopped by the Enders home on two separate occasions after the birth in order to ensure the well-being of the twins, now part of an awkward quartet with a wine-soaked mother and a theoretical physicist father, the latter who was often too absorbed in his work to come home for days on end. She scribbled notes for Family Services with derision next to a full kitchen sink.

Had Victoire not passed a rigorous civil service exam and been promoted to Family Liaison Officer, Level Three, she surely would not have even come across the opportunity to influence the destiny of the Enders to such a degree. But she took her newfound powers of decision seriously. Victoire dismissed comments that her title was merely for administrative purposes and ignored the mockery that ensued while she stenciled "Level Three" onto her door in a move of unadulterated professional pride.

After moving downtown and receiving yet another fantastic promotion, Victoire Lambert once again crossed paths with the Enders twins. She had been haunted by the mother's apparent lack of compassion and was hardly surprised to learn that Claire had left her family a few years down the line. But the father's self-mutilating behavior with a power tool had taken her off guard. She had visited the newly single father just two months earlier and found them to be getting by, even if it was not the most conventional household. Victoire had potentially failed these children in the past by signing off on the Enders, letting them slip out of the system of checks and balances that she had so come to believe in as she had climbed ranks to Family Liaison Officer, Level Four.

So when the news came that the twins were abruptly without parental supervision, Victoire fudged paperwork with an artistry that only an officer with level four status could appreciate. Victoire knew she'd done the best for the family. But even now as a retired Level Five atop a snowy hill in the country of her birth, she thought of the Enders girls from time to time. She almost called it fate when her phone rang and the sing-song voice of Doctor Vicky found her at last. He was concerned about a patient of his, he'd explained. His patient had lost his children over twenty years ago and he'd been living in a mental institution to this day.

A barrage of questions floated like music through the line. Did she know where the children were? Could she help in some way? But, ma'am, the situation is very dire, you must understand. Yes, I understand that files are confidential. No, I didn't know you were retired. Still, please Ms. Lambert, do you know where the children are? I am trying to grasp the responsibility you must feel at level five clearance. Yes, I'm aware that it must be a very important classification and I congratulate you on your advancement as a civil servant, but, please, the children? Where are the Enders children? No, I haven't filled out that form and I—please, ma'am, this is—I need your help. Can you repeat that number? No, I don't wish to file any, Ms. Lambert, I need to find those children very soon. Yes, I respect procedures too. No, I'm not being curt. Yes, I—. No, I—. Yes, ma'am, I—please, Victoire, you gave one of them your name. Carl trusted you. Please let him find his children. No, I wasn't aware, but…no, I'm sorry I can't…no, I'm quite sorry, but it's too far and I don't have time to…yes, but…yes, Ms. Lambert. I'm on my way.

The next day Viswanatha Suresh Venkataraman was stomping the snow off his boots in front of Victoire's door.

Victoire had unremarkable features that were exaggerated by dark makeup. Round eyes rimmed with black, thin lips stained burgundy and pale skin that showed the lines of the brush used to apply rouge in long strokes down her otherwise unapparent cheekbones. She was dressed in several blacks: a dark, synthetic top with a sheen and fading cotton black, nearly gray, on her trousers. Her hair was the deep, saturated hue that can only be achieved by more than one box of home hair dye. Her whole look seemed to imply a forced sternness that could only come naturally after decades of pretending. She invited the doctor in and looked at his feet with a raised eyebrow that was obviously a command. Suresh removed his boots and tiptoed carefully in giant white tube socks around the puddle the melting snow was making. The floor matched the walls, knotty pine wood that enhanced the warm yellowy glow from the fireplace. In fact the whole room was pine, from the cupboards to the tables and even the paneled ceiling. The cozy home matched neither the exterior, with its all-weather aluminum siding, nor its owner. Dr. Vicky felt as if he'd walked through a carnival door.

"Oat drink?" she asked the Doctor. Her French-Canadian accent had come back in full force since retirement and Suresh realized she was offering him warm liquid when she repeated, "Somezing oat to drink?" He nodded and sat down close to the flames.

Victoire cut the corner off a block of butter on the countertop and slid it down into a clay mug, scraping the knife on the side. She then dipped below the counter until just her black bun was visible and rummaged through the lower cupboards. When she came back up, she was holding a bottle of whiskey and a jug of maple syrup. Dr. Vicky stared incredulously as she poured them into a metal pan and walked over to the fire. He hadn't seen it before, but there was a tiny, cast iron shelf sticking out from the fireplace, the perfect size for a saucepan. The syrupy whiskey started to bubble on the fire as Victoire opened a bottle of red wine and held the cork up to her nose, taking a deep, even breath. She took the hot pan and poured it into the mug, melting the butter and stirring with the knife, then topped it off with red wine and handed it to Dr. Vicky. "Caribou Lambert. My father's recipe." Dr. Vicky looked doubtfully into his mug, the butter forming little spheres that looked like primitive eyes on the surface of the winter punch. It was surprisingly good. One Caribou became three as the unlikely pair talked on a dark green cushion atop a knotty pine bench and Suresh recounted the last three months he'd spent with Carl Enders.

What Dr. Vicky had seen the first time peering into Carl's twinkling grey eyes was a partial clouding that came with a type of slow-growing, but untreatable, brain tumor. He had confirmed with a scan that he had brought along to show Victoire, but it now seemed inappropriate so he just described it, the warmth of the Caribou pushing the words out. The headaches and delusions that Carl had experienced as a young father had been the first nudge from the invading growth. Strangely, the artificial limbo that Carl had entered as a drugged and forgotten patient had significantly slowed the growth of the tumor. The time gained, of course, had been lost again to a meaningless life, but Dr. Vicky took it as a sign that Carl was meant to meet his grown daughters, adults now who could only hope to know him for a quick second beginning and an even quicker end.

He wanted to know everything Victoire knew about Carl, everything she knew about his children. Dr. Vicky was not here for lawyers or revenge. He sat back on the pine couch, letting his head rest in the carved-out heart shape of the back, and left room in the air for Victoire to speak. He was either used to her accent now or it had disappeared like his inhibitions, washed away by Caribou.

"Carl Enders came to me when the mother left. Said that he couldn't take care of them, that he didn't know how to braid hair, stuff like that. He said he was better at hot air balloon rides than combing out snarls. He didn't seem like he was going to kill himself, he just wanted help with the girls. I did a home visit, wrote a report. Sure enough, he had a giant basket in his basement, big enough for 4 people to climb into. There was this film strip that he'd project on the wall to make it look like landscapes were rushing by below. I even went for a ride with the girls. Carl blew a fan on our faces as I stood in the basket and looked at that wall. It was fun, actually, almost like the real thing. Well, I've never been on a real balloon ride, but I imagine it would be like that.

"Carl's place was full of odd things. I remember beaters, you know attachments for hand mixers? They were hanging from the ceiling on long strings all over the house. I asked what they were for and he just said they were for mixing. Also, he had framed sheets of striped Christmas gift wrap and used them as art. And the girls' room! He had painted it like a forest and stapled leaves to the ceiling. There were artificial trees in there, even a monkey that hung over one of the beds. It was a bit over-the-top, really. But you could see that he loved them. You could see that, you really could.

"He hadn't told the girls anything yet about their mother's disappearance and he didn't know what to say. Didn't know what to do. His wife had

22

found out that Carl was seeing someone on the side, someone from his lab. I honestly thought she'd be back. He didn't. I asked when he'd last seen her and he said it was next to the ball pit at Playland. So, I suggested telling the girls that their mother got lost in the balls, that was it was nobody's fault. If she came back, she could just say she found her way out and what a relief it was, etc. They were small; they couldn't possibly understand. I mean, they believed they were going on hot air balloon rides every morning.

"But I was wrong. I was wrong and she didn't come back. Carl knew she had left for good and he did something drastic, something meant to be irreversible. His children were home at the time, did you know that? His daughter, Laney, found him sticking a drill in his brain. Can you imagine that? Can you? It must have been awful for her.

"I wanted to save those girls, save Laney. They had a better chance of getting adopted as singles anyway. It's hard enough to place one older child, not to mention two. And Laney would have felt inferior her whole life. Her sister, Vicky, was the smiley one, the talkative one, the one that everyone paid attention to. Did you know they called her Superman? I mean, how was Laney supposed to keep up with Superman? It wasn't fair. I gave them both a chance by splitting them up. I gave two four year-olds a chance at parents that wanted them, families that loved them.

"I redacted their birth certificates, making them each singletons. I even gave them the same name: Victoria Laney Enders. For all practical purposes, they're the same person, just placed in two different county systems. Laney was adopted right away by a family with the name Victoria. Obviously they didn't want a Victoria Victoria so they were happy to call her Laney. It was a win-win. I met the family. They're fantastically rich, fantastically happy. Fantastic. I didn't follow Vicky, the other daughter, because she was out of my jurisdiction, but I'm sure she found a fantastic family too. She would have been the easier of the two to place. Much brighter. I don't even mean intelligent, but really brighter, like sunlight. Laney was a child with a dark cloud over her; the Victorias were the best thing that ever happened to her.

"I listed their mother as deceased, by the way, in their files. Since she was supposedly wading aimlessly in a ball pit I called it a drowning. Yes, I let her drown. I needed to. I knew at that point what Carl had known before the incident, that she really wasn't coming back. My team cleared out over 900 empty wine bottles from the cellar of that house after Carl was committed. And Carl didn't drink, if you know what I'm saying. She definitely wasn't going to come looking for them. No one was. To be honest, before you called, I believed that Carl was dead. I didn't think someone could survive the kind of damage he did to himself for very long.

"If he's really alive and aware, I still don't imagine he knows how long it's been. The girls must be almost 30 by now. Let's see, no, 28. They'd be 28. Do you really think it's the best for them to meet Carl now?"

CARLOS
(2004)

Upon return from his otherworldly meeting with Victoire Lambert, Suresh walked quietly into his apartment so as not to disturb Carl. After his dramatic renaissance from the mental hospital, Carl's tumor had reawakened and started taking over in unpredictable ways. Suresh pressed $500 into the temporary nurse's palm and thanked her for her overnight watch as he walked her to the door. He paused to look at a photo of a sad-eyed woman in a sari next to the door frame as he let the nurse out, and with one heart beat contemplated a life that would have been.

The last two months had provided intense conversation, but also invaluable observation, for Dr. Vicky. He could see firsthand the effects of the growing mass as it pioneered new territory in Carl's skull. Parts of his body would tremble and then become momentarily paralyzed before returning to life in jerky fits. Sometimes he'd swear he could smell numbers and letters. As his vision grew cloudier, Suresh would help him more and more with tasks like shaving and making breakfast, until the day he woke up to find that he was completely blind. But he'd still feel his way into the kitchen, swearing he could smell baking cookies, just so he could feel the cold oven door and then go back to bed.

Carl woke several times during the night, sometimes waking up Suresh too as he ran into furniture or dropped pans. On several occasions the tumor's reach activated poetry he'd learned and forgotten as a young student, which would methodically pace out of Carl's mouth in his sleep. Dr. Vicky now tiptoed to the side of Carl's couch bed as he spoke.

> I fear thee ancient mariner, I fear thy skinny hand
> And thou art long and lank and lean as is the ribbed sea sand.

25

I fear thee and thy glittering eye, and thy skinny hand so brown.
Fear not, fear not, thou Wedding-Guest! This body dropped not down.

He held Carl's hand, for the first and only time since the hospital, as his brain continued regurgitating memories before letting them go.

Alone, alone, all, all alone, alone on a wide, wide sea
And never a saint took pity on my soul in agony.

Suresh kept Carl's hand in his through two more sections of *The Rime of the Ancient Mariner* before the cycles switched to silent and Carl's eyelids stopped flittering through dreams. The next morning they would take their weekly ride on Suresh's imported Lambretta, something Carl was intensely excited about, but Suresh wanted this moment in the low light of his living room to last a bit longer. He vowed to take as many possible of Carl's lost memories as his own and made a mental note to buy a Coleridge analogy in the near future.

Carl awoke with no recollection of Dr. Vicky's company nor their plans to have a picnic and ride. He took the news with delight and rejected Suresh's insistence that he wear a helmet. "Let an old man air out a bit, will you, Doctor?" he said with a grin when he was reminded that the soft spot on his head should especially be protected before his big reunion with Vicky and Laney the next day. They packed a lentil salad—Carl had been won over by the Venkataraman style of eating nothing with a face—and set out on Suresh's motorcycle.

The air blowing through Carl's hair felt perfect. It was a different kind of pressure from the grey that had haunted him in his youth and its unpredictable change in direction was like therapy. He could feel the shadows on his skin as they passed under shade trees, flickering heat, cool, heat and cool. Carl allowed his ever-wandering mind to wander even more as he held onto Dr. Vicky's grand torso. His arms reminded him that they too had once loved and held someone tight. There was a great bump and without feeling himself let go, Carl was flying. He seemed both to be soaring and lying still at the same time. He could hear Suresh yelling, "Carl! Carl!" Even his shouting was sing-song pleasant.

Suresh had swerved and slid after a near-miss with a passing car that had ejected Carl and sent him rolling off to the side of the road in a flurry of brown dust. He unpinned himself from under the motorcycle, threw his helmet off and limped to where Carl now lay face up on the ground. He was motionless and smiling faintly; he looked like a stargazer in full daylight. Suresh didn't grab Carl's hand as he screamed his name for fear it would be the last time. He instead took Carl's head between his two hands, framing his face and the grey eyes that looked right through him, no longer shining now, but covered with a milky blur. He spoke to Dr. Vicky using a name from lifetimes ago, one Suresh had only seen in Victoire's file.

"Yes, yes, I'm here. I'm here, Carlos. I found it. It's the most beautiful green. Not a hint of red, not a trace of blue. It's perfect."

Suresh called back, still shouting, "What do you see, Carl? Can you see?"

"No, Carlos," Carl replied with a broader smile than before. "I can't hear it either. I can smell it. It smells just like chocolate cake." And the smile went slack in slow motion as Carl escaped the pressure of his world.

*

Suresh's doctor allowed him to travel to Mexico for the funeral, but he needed a cane, making him look much older than his 48 years. Dr. Vicky knew he had to go, not only to pay his respects, but to live up to the guilt of making Carl miss his appointment with his two daughters. They would be there, he knew they would.

At the cemetery an assortment of Catholic villagers cried and swayed for the man they had either never known or had gotten a glimpse of as a young boy. They held up Mrs. Méndez, the wailing mother, as she gripped a rosary and white flowers. A woman wrapped in a teal paisley scarf and oversized glasses stood far behind the group, trying to look anonymous, but her other accessory, an impeccably dressed Senator, gave her away.

The other Enders daughter arrived in a parade of young women who bore little resemblance to one another apart from their black hair and varying degrees of disabilities, making Suresh feel guiltier still that his cane was only temporary. They gathered around the burial site, one of them being pushed in a hot pink wheelchair by a woman with the same pewter eyes that Suresh had stared into the week before.

LANEY
(1980)

Mr. and Mrs. Lothaire Victoria had adopted the off-centered nymph at age four. They'd heard there would be problems with Laney, but they sought inspiration in her friendly grey eyes and waited patiently for the child to speak. Along with a suggestion that the girl loved candy that looked like medicine, the only information provided pertained to her father, a colorful character who had a penchant for drilling holes in his head. There had been no mention of a twin sister throughout the adoption process and only after months of coaxing did a tidy little hum escape from Laney as she swept her dolls over a braided rug. Sound. The humming continued for weeks before Laney pronounced the name of her missing other half, only to be met by encouraging smiles of her new parents, who tried to help clear up the confusion. "Laney, dear. Your name is Laney." As the years leaked by, Laney forgot her sister, but the night played tricks on her. Imaginary friends took the name Vicky and friendly animals came to pace at the foot of her bed in the moments between sleep and wake. A luminescent blue fox whispered *Vicky, Vicky.* Her sleep-fogged brain insisted on twirling the name around, weaving it into dreams for decades to come.

*

The Victorias had worked hard and made a small fortune by engineering and patenting vending machines. Lothaire twice had to sue former business partners for full rights to the design, but in doing so became solely responsible for the liabilities associated with the machines. In a grievous oversight, the insurance was not properly carried over when Minvin Machines became L. M. Victoria Co. and the emerging empire was stopped in its tracks as an Olympic ice skater altered the Victoria destiny. The skater had been on tour and visiting an all-night laundromat equipped with one of

Lothaire's creations. While trying to wrangle a bag of chips that dangled tauntingly over a ledge of snacks, the skater's arm became hopelessly wedged in the machine. A team of firefighters gave it their all; the ice skater's arm was amputated at the elbow.

Lothaire's lawyers tried unconvincingly to demonstrate that it was, in fact, the legs that were important to ice skating, not the arms. Each legal team paraded across the courtroom, simulating double axles that either benefitted or suffered from the partial absence of a limb, but the judge found that a hand was indeed helpful for balance, not to mention artistic flair. Lothaire Victoria, uninsured and solely responsible for his monster, signed the judgment that bound him to a lifetime of incapacity payments for the young star whose light who would no longer shine so brightly.

The contents of the Victoria home were carried away by various repossession teams, leaving nowhere to sit, but ample room for Laney to run. What they lacked in toys and furniture, Lothaire and Minnie made up for in their patient parenting. When Laney's head hurt, they gave her powdery orange chewable pills. They told stories and had picnics on the living room floor. They read from the expansive collection of leatherbound books that were lined up shelfless along the wall, inventing a game called "Sages of the Ages" that involved reading passages with overdone foreign accents. When the last of the books was carted away, they went to the library and often stayed until closing time, each Victoria quite content in his or her section.

Laney was less interested in books than her parents, but found that you could check out all sorts of things from the library, from puppets to telescopes. She once came home with a bundt cake pan, just because she felt sorry that it hadn't been checked out in years. She gave puppet shows to her invisible friend and sister, Vicky, in the empty house.

After four years, Lothaire and Minnie clinked glasses of champagne together in the kitchen as quietly as possible. The ice skater had been in another freak accident, this time losing her life, in essence freeing L. M. Victoria Co. from its bondage. One by one, the works of art returned. One painting, a Jackson Pollack, especially captivated Laney. Her father insisted it was the even distribution of color that was pleasing to the eye, but Laney saw another form of beauty in the desperate paint configuration that made her want to hold tight onto her father in the hallway.

One day, when her second family was the only one she could remember, Mr. Victoria took Laney on his knee and told her a story of a little girl who was left under a tree in a land far away. The land she lived in had no more room for little girls and the Victorias had a big, big house. Lothaire asked if they should invite the girl to come live with them. Laney had so many questions. Was it a Christmas tree that she was found under? Was her name Vicky? Would she belong to Laney?

"Sweetheart, she'll be part of our family. And she'll be your sister." The whole family boarded a plane, crossed several time zones, and returned with Ping. Out of guilt for the skater, Lothaire had specifically requested an orphan with a missing limb. Laney liked to carry the one-legged girl around and feed her tiny round pebbles in the back garden. Laney called the pebbles her pills and she only shared them with people she truly loved. Ping was soon Laney's favorite person in the world and she would do anything to protect her.

Lothaire and Laney ceremoniously threw Ping's wheelchair into a dumpster one day at the beach, insisting she get more practice with her new prosthetic limb and crutches. Sunburned brats would point at Ping by the lakeshore and whisper. Laney charged into the waves with her sister and taught her to swim. Years later, Ping would be the first one-legged lifeguard in the upper Midwest, but for now she had to practice holding her breath and having underwater tea parties with Laney.

The Victorias were financially successful, but out of wall space for art, so they resorted to collecting more children. When Ping and Laney were both nine, Lothaire sat them both down on beanbag chairs and told them that Hua and Li-Hua would be arriving soon. These new twins were also from a faraway land, and needed an operation in an American hospital to separate them into two bodies. Ping was immediately jealous when the twins arrived and Laney shared her pebbles with them. By the time chubby little Meilen arrived a year later, the rock garden was nearly empty. Laney had to scrounge around in the bushes to find pebbles for Jade, her youngest sister who incidentally had no arms.

Although Laney knew she wasn't supposed to have a favorite, Ping was her sister of choice. The two could talk without speaking and fight without touching. They were connected at a more fundamental level than the other sisters and Laney knew immediately when Ping began to slide into sadness.

Mr. and Mrs. Victoria were not originally as concerned as Laney, who saw Ping's bouncy gait turn into a laborious affair of dragging her plastic leg like dead weight. It was Laney who felt a wet pillow on her cheek as Ping cried silently by her side each night. And it was Laney who kept a chart in her notebook to document how often she saw the dimple in Ping's left cheek, a dimple that only came out when Ping smiled. It had been three weeks since she'd last ticked a box on the chart.

Ping's low spirits first became apparent to her parents with Minnie's Shakespeare test. On tenth birthdays, she made each of her daughters pick a sonnet as a window into her character. Laney eagerly latched onto a passage rife with science:

> Not from the stars do I my judgement pluck,
> And yet methinks I have astronomy,

But pigtailed Ping, whose birthday followed a week later, crossed her arms in defiance as her little sister Jade looked on in wonder. Jade never crossed her arms. Ping read in a low voice from memory:

> No longer mourn for me when I am dead,
> Than you shall hear the surly sullen bell
> Give warning to the world that I am fled
> From this vile world with vilest worms to dwell.

By this time the Victoria family counted eight souls, but only seven who were enthusiastic about being alive. Laney knew she had to help her glum sibling on their next family outing. After three hours at the Quatchik County library, Laney piled into the wide handicapped-accessible van with her sisters and a book, *Mastering your Universe* by Victor Su, that would save Ping.

VICTOR SU
(1986)

Laney read the book twice before going through the complicated procedure of transferring her sister's darkness to herself. She was sure it would work, especially since Mr. Su had also been exported from Ping's country of birth and seemed to be very authoritative on the subject of the universe. Laney wanted nothing more than to take away the pain that would otherwise crush her dear Ping under its weight.

The actual ceremony involved lemons, ginger, cardboard tubes, a mirror and vinegar. But most importantly it included a great deal of chanting, something Laney wasn't accustomed to, but found easy in the shade of the back garden, which a dump truck had thankfully replenished with pebbles the previous summer.

Mr. Su strongly encouraged personalizing the chants. Laney looked into the mirror at the space just over her shoulder and repeated 99 times, "Give me your sadness, sister. I take it as my own." The name she'd never really remembered, but refused to forget, came pulsing back. While Ping's dark hair and teary eyes came into focus, Vicky's name did too.

Minnie and Lothaire laughed as they paged through Laney's library book later that night. They had brought dear Ping to a competent doctor who had prescribed the most beautiful green pills and they were convinced that things would be better for their daughter from now on.

And as Ping's dimple came back, the Victorias knew that they were right.
On her 18th birthday, Mr. and Mrs. Victoria gave Laney, their yin-burdened eldest, a fancy camera and the gift of a new start. They clasped their

33

daughter's hands as she sat in a county office, legally changing her name to Vicky Victoria.

VICKY
(2003)

A now 27-year-old and still relatively taciturn Vicky was leading herself on a journey to try any drugs she could procure in her dullish neighborhood. This usually ended up being a derivative of cough medicine or unidentified pills from the pizza man. It would sometimes be enough to make her forget all the effort she had put into forgetting, allowing her to wake to the bliss of an empty mind. But her photography was turning shades darker by the day, focusing on unskilled graffiti and the undersides of bridges. Pigeon poop made its way into several compositions. A greyish thudding sensation wouldn't escape her brain for more than a few seconds at a time and each click of the camera shutter seemed to increase the pressure in her head.

Vicky needed to calm the pulsing behind her eyes, so she rummaged through her home pharmacy before the afternoon's job of capturing pseudo-celebrities on film. The combination of four different, but reassuringly legal, potions brought the thumping to a halt, but left her fingertips numb. Vicky questioned her desire to see anymore tomorrows as she walked to work, snapping shots of litter-filled puddles along the way.

There was a jolt of recognition, accompanied by the most stereo of sounds. Millions of colors moved in pinstripes, churning but never mixing, in every direction she looked.

A wordless comprehension of the universe engulfed Vicky for a precious moment, with a lifetime sliding forward and back to a little blue fox at the foot of her bed, then cruelly robbed her of the vocabulary to describe what she'd experienced. And then, as surely as she'd discovered the meaning of Everything, it was gone. Vicky rubbed her eyes and continued on her path.

This seemed to be a day of optical illusions because minutes later the couple she was scheduled to photograph appeared and the wife looked too familiar to be coincidence. She was tied up in an elaborate silk scarf, but her face was like an illumination. Vicky was transfixed-she couldn't move as she stood, head cocked to one side, admiring the burst of light that had crossed her path.

The woman reached out a hand and Vicky took it limply in her own. "Have we met somewhere before?" asked the brightness.

"Vicky Victoria. And no, I think I'd remember you," she replied.

The woman had invited her for coffee, which was a moment Laney preferred to forget. She had felt a spark that made her reach for the woman, but there was no connection. All of Laney's electrons had bounced out gracelessly onto the table as the substantially more beautiful version of Laney refused to complete the circuit. She felt shame now as she remembered suggesting they were sisters.

But one year later, there was a message on her phone from Dr. Venkataraman that made the corners of her mouth turn up. She hadn't been wrong; that woman was another sister. And even stranger, she had another father. One that had brought her on hot air balloon rides and made her grilled cheese sandwiches. Didn't she remember? They would meet again tomorrow. Her birth father still loved her, the doctor had said with a lightness that rang bells. Vicky loved his voice.

CLAIRE
(2003)

She was formerly known as Mrs. Méndez. And before that she was Miss Viereck. But now she was just the elegant yet eccentric Claire, brushing up on her Swahili grammar and Russian calligraphy. She sipped the second cheapest wine on the menu and reassured herself for the thousandth time that she had done the right thing by leaving those girls, their tangled hair, their chapped lips, their sticky hands and their clumsy feet.

It's not supposed to be easy to leave your family, but for Claire it had been comfortingly so. As her husband pressed his hands to his temples and her two toddlers played in a writhing mass of colorful, urine-scented plastic balls, Claire had watched the shaft of light at the back of the room. It meant there was something beyond those greasy walls and gleefully screaming children. It meant escape. Since anchoring her purse over her shoulder and beginning the deliberate march toward the streak of light in the back, Claire Enders had never looked back.

The newly independent Claire liked to mix together different combinations of perfume. She liked to travel. She liked to make cakes. Sometimes the batter would accidentally slip out of the big pan and make its way into two smaller ones, baking itself into two perfect little rounds. In moments like these she had no choice but to decorate them with tiny frosting rosebuds and daisies, then steady her trembling hands to squirt out a cursive L and V before lovingly nestling the little cakes into the trash.

*

Now 24 years later and two tables over were twin sisters who could easily have been Laney and Vicky. Any time Claire saw twins, they looked like hers, but these ones even had the puffy nose and twinkling eyes of her husband from another life. *See*, she thought, *those girls are fine. Look how long they've been hugging.* The two young women walked right by her table, which was covered in texts of non-Latin alphabets, before going separate directions. *Yes, at least they had each other*, Claire thought for a few seconds until she remembered to make her way back to memorize a Hopi wedding song.

*

(2010)

When Claire returned home from a tour of the Amazon almost a decade later, she noticed the folded newspaper on the kitchen table. She had hesitated to drop it in the recycling bin that morning because of the color photo of Senator Vickie and his wife. She pulled some scissors out of the kitchen drawer to clip around the edges of what had caught her eye. *I just have to find a scarf like that.* But the burgundy scarf drifted lazily down to the mosaic of tiles that Claire had grouted herself in a series of all-night solo maintenance parties. On the back of the scarf was a want ad:

AUNT VICKY
(2010)

-So whose aunt are you, Aunt Vicky?

Don't got any siblings, can't be nobody's auntie, child.

-So, just "Vicky"?

Naw, Vicky just a nickname.

-So, what do I call you?

You call me Aunt Vicky. That's what you do.

-So, why should I call you something you aren't?

Why you gotta start every sentence with 'so'? Maybe you's named me Aunt Vicky. Help you remember.

-But your ad says "Aunt Vicky" in the clairvoyant section. You put the ad there, not me.

I done place hundreds of ads with hundreds of names. Venture to say most of yous find exactly what you come lookin' for that way. You think I'm clairvoyant? That's a good one, child. That's a good one. I like that quite much, dear. You be looking for Aunt Vicky. Aunt Vicky is here, child.

-So, all your hundreds of ads have the same phone number? Doesn't that look suspicious?

There you go with the 'so' again. How many people you know go analyzin' the want ads all day? Don't you worry 'bout my phones, my names. You tell me what color them apples are in front of you and we get somewhere.

Claire Enders picked up a red apple from the bowl that sat on the table in the narrow space between Aunt Vicky and herself. She rubbed off the waxy coating on her shirt and took several large bites. She wiped her mouth with her sleeve and not an ounce of elegance.

-It's red, Aunt Vicky.

The world around you has no color, child. This apple be tellin' you it's red because it's bouncin' some wavelengths at your eyeballs. Aint a thing red about this apple. Take another bite, Claire.

Claire paused. Had she mentioned her name?

-That's ridiculous.

Not only that apple's not red. Not even there, that apple. You thinkin' you see it cause it's throwin' that light to you, child. Sendin' messages to your eyes. To the backs of your eyes. Your eyes is part of your brain, you know.

Aunt Vicky's eyebrows shot up as she said "brain."

-So, you're some kind of fourth grade science teacher, Miss Vicky? Excuse me, Aunt Vicky. I hope you don't think I'm paying for this consultation. I'm not paying for your corny accent either. And I'm 63 so you can stop with the "child" part as well.

All I'm sayin' is the apple aint here. Apple not here, I'm not here. Can't be worryin' about payments and such if I'm not even here, child.

-So, I guess I'll be going now. Thanks for the apple, Aunt Vicky. Claire hesitated at the door.

Sound aint a thing either. Just be waves ticklin' your ears, bouncin' off something else. Only that something aint there either. That something just made up of smaller things and smaller things and when you get too close you see they aint even things, they just movin'. They just patterns. Ridin' around on little tracks.

Aunt Vicky moved her hand up and down like it was going over a tiny roller coaster.

But the tracks aint there either, child. Whole lot of nothin' to be bouncin' things back.

-So, unkempt philosopher meets grammatically inept scam artist? Thanks for the life lesson, Vic. I can't say I'm really impressed.

SO, said Aunt Vicky with a huff and a readjustment of her ample backside, *if the world aint what it seems, then why it seem the way it does?* She pointed at Claire for effect, a gesture that annoyed her, but provoked a response and a rush of blood to her cheeks.

-Because…because I did make it all up? Because you're not really here? Because I never had a husband or children. Because I'm not an 'International Lifelong Learner' like my resume on Monster says. I don't do wine tastings and learn Arabic prose. I'm not even here.

If you say so, child. If you say so.

-So, how does it all end? I mean, if the world doesn't exist and I don't exist, how does it end?

With marimba music, sugar. It'll fall right out them clouds.

MARKA
(2010)

Claire awoke in a haze. She wasn't sure if her conversation with Aunt Vicky was a dream or the product of a late date with a second bottle of wine. She knew what she had to do to understand. She drank a small glass of courage in the form of pinot griggio and looked up Marka Swandish, her former husband's regretful muse.

"Yeah?" answered a young male voice at the lab, yelling over a loud thumping noise.

"Hello, I'm looking for Carl Enders. Is he available, please?"

"Just a minute…Marka? Marka! Someone's looking for Fat Carl."

There was an audible click and the thumping stopped. The clopping of heavy heels came and a woman picked up the phone.

"Hello? This is Marka Swandish."

"Ms. Swandish, my name is Claire. I'm looking for Carl Enders."

"You mean Fat Carl?"

"Well, no. I'm looking for Dr. Enders, the physicist. He worked in your lab around 1980."

"Yeah, Fat Carl. He was here for a few years, but that was a long time ago. I think he went back to Mexico with his family."

Claire had spent the last few decades believing Carl was living with Marka, the woman who had tickled his brain in all the right ways before Claire left and yet here she was, calling him Fat Carl and clearly no longer involved with him. She felt foolish for not even considering Mexico, Carl's first home and the place they'd met. He'd stopped going by Carlos before the girls were born and only spoke Spanish once a year when he'd call his mother on New Year's Day. His sparkly grey eyes made most people forget that he used to be Carlos Méndez.

"Carl was pretty skinny when I knew him…he was…he's…I'm his wife, Claire."

There was a nasal laughter on the end of the line. "It was just to tell them apart, you know. Kind of a joke because the other Carlos was actually fatter than him."

"The other Carlos?"

"Well, yeah, there were two guys in the lab named Carlos. Anyway, you said you're his wife? I don't get it. Why are you calling me?"

"I…I thought maybe you and Carl lived together. You know, because of your history and everything? I need to find him."

"Look, Mrs. Enders? I haven't seen Fat Carl in a very long time. When you left, he stopped coming to work, said he needed a big change. I talked to him on the phone once and then he just dropped off the radar. He never even came for his stuff. I figured you guys got back together. I looked him up a few times to see if he was publishing. I tried Enders and Méndez, but there was nothing, which is why I figured he was back in Mexico." After a long pause she said, "Maybe you should call the police."

Claire could think of nothing else to say. She had always assumed that Carl would be exactly where she left him, playing house with this bitch scientist. "Mrs. Enders, why don't you come by the lab? I still have some things of Carl's here. Claire? Are you still there?"

"Yes, Marka. But it's Méndez, Claire Méndez. Yes. I'll come." Claire glanced at the current bottle of wine and was confident that more than half remained. She wouldn't be driving with one eye closed today. "I'll come right now," she added before hanging up.

*

It took her three hours by car. The address she'd been given was not the university lab Carl and Marka had worked at in the eighties. Dr. Swandish's workplace was not even how Claire had expected a lab to look. Everyone was dressed in jeans and sitting on couches; nary a soul ran by in a white coat. Most of them were hunched over clunky laptops. Claire wore a security badge given to her by an attendant and tried to find her way to Marka.

One minute later a great, rectangular woman pounded down the corridor in high heels—finally someone in a lab coat. Claire stared long enough to evoke the physicist's first line. "I'm a few shades darker than you expected?" Claire knew Marka Swandish was born in Nigeria so her complexion was not a surprise, but her hair was a massive, ragged sphere of grey that dominated the room.

"Your hair—" started Claire before Marka reached out to shake her hand.

"Yes, I'm a regular black Einstein. Please don't touch it. I hate when people touch my hair."

She was at least six feet tall and broad enough to block doorways. Her perfectly symmetrical brown face was both beautiful and mismatched to her hulking frame. Marka led Claire down another long hallway that made her feel claustrophobic with its lack of natural light. "The server room," offered Marka and then continued with a story about the donuts that Fat Carl used to bring to work.

They finally emerged into an archive room crammed with tables and floor-to-ceiling shelves, all overstocked with piles of yellowing paper and folders. "Carl's over here," she said and led Claire to a shelf that sagged in the middle from the weight of its paper burden. "This is everything he was working on when he left."

Claire picked up a stapled document from the top of the pile and read the title aloud. "Chasing the Supergreen Dragon: Simulating Impossible Colors."

"I think people read his papers, but in a wink-wink, nudge-nudge kind of way. I think Bostrom read Carl and clarified what he meant." Marka handed her a folio by Carl entitled 'Yes, you are Living in a Simulation.'

"Bostrom?"

"A Swede. He was probably in kindergarten when Carl first published. He's a much better speaker than Carl. Also more logical. But he's using the same premise. He describes it as a set of 3 propositions."

"I'm sorry, I don't follow."

Marka sighed. "Three possibilities. Like three little pigs: house of hay, house of sticks, house of bricks."

"No, I know what the number 3 means, but I don't know what Carl's work was about." There. She had summed up her persistent lack of interest in her husband's life in one sentence. She looked cautiously at Marka, expecting to be chastised, but instead Marka just glanced at her watch as though she was considering whether to waste her time with Claire.

"Have a seat," said Marka, motioning to her right. Claire saw neither a chair nor anything that could double as one so she sat on the floor in the middle of the stacks. Marka squatted next to her, hovering a few inches above the floor. "This used to be a natural human position, you know." And Claire couldn't help but laugh as the giant 70 year-old squatted next to her, with elbows on her knees. Carl had mentioned the same thing dozens of times and was often found reading in the squat position for hours on end. He'd insisted the girls do the same whenever they tried to sit cross-legged like they'd been advised in preschool.

"I know, Marka. I know." Dr. Swandish smiled genuinely at Claire and patted her on the knee. It almost felt grandmotherly, but this woman could only have been 10 years older than Claire, and her youthful face made the gesture seem awkward.

"Well, there are basically three possibilities, the way Bostrom sees it. Carl didn't phrase it this way, but it makes the most sense to people. Yes, so the first possibility is that no human civilization will ever be capable of performing a simulation that is complex enough to act as a reality for what is embedded in the simulation. A reality for the sims, if you like."

"The sims? Like Sim City?"

"Like Sim City or any other program, projection, whatever you want to call it. A simulated creation with things going on, people carrying on lives, cause and effect relationships. A sense of space."

"It sounds like that movie, The Matrix."

"Yes, that's one way to look at it. But we don't have to be ruled by computers to get there; that just makes for a good story. A simulation could be just an advanced form of virtual reality, an enhanced 3-D movie, anything like that. Anyway, the first supposition is that a Matrix-type scenario is impossible, that humans will never have the capacity of creating a sufficiently simulated existence."

"So you and Carl thought it was impossible? Even with computers getting faster, Moore's Law and all that?"

"Moore's Law! Claire, why didn't you ever talk to your husband? He loved Moore's Law. Loved it. And no one even talked about it back when I knew him. No one except Carl. He was religious about the doubling of processor power, he thought it would lead to exponential artificial intelligence."

"Well, I just read about it recently for a night class. Anyway, Carl and I didn't really have a lot in common when we lived together. It was like we didn't speak the same language, even cross paths in our daily life."

"Well you actually didn't speak the same language in the beginning, right?"

"Of course we did! I couldn't go beyond ordering enchiladas in Spanish back then." Claire didn't mention that she had spent over two years hiking around South America and was now close to fluent, despite having an over-represented vocabulary of local sugar-cane spirits. "Carl and I spoke English from the time we met. And he hated when I called him Carlos. Carl's father picked lettuce for awhile in California and then he sent Carl to a school for American brats in Mexico City. He was convinced that his only son would have a better life if he spoke English. Carl didn't even have an accent. He always joked that his father had robbed a bank to pay for that school."

"Did he?" said Marka with a chuckle. "Rob a bank, I mean?"

"Who knows? I don't know. I never really knew anything about his family. He never talked about them. When he was naturalized, he changed his name to Enders. The whole thing was ridiculous because I had already taken his name when we got married. So I was more Méndez than him." Claire stopped there with another omission: that she'd always feared Carl only married her to get his citizenship. She'd spent over 30 years trying to convince the world that she was interesting enough to wed, and in doing so was more alone than ever.

Marka thankfully circled back to her previous topic. "Anyway, the first possibility is that no simulations are technologically possible, right? Well, the second says that they are possible, but that no human civilization would ever perform them."

"Why?"

"The 'why' is actually not important. The essential point is that humans don't perform simulations. Or any other civilizations, aliens or whatever you want to imagine. They didn't run full-scale simulations before, they don't do it now and they won't ever in the future. Even if they were capable."

"But why? I mean, why wouldn't they?"

"It's just a possibility. It's a possibility that provides comfort, resolution. It simplifies things. Because if it's not true, then you go to possibility three."

"Which is?"

"That we are most definitely living in a simulation."

Claire implored Marka to continue, not seeing the connection.

"If civilizations are capable of creating high-quality simulations and even one of them decides to go through with it, then they are essentially simulating a civilization like their own, one that is equally capable of running a simulation. When you line up two mirrors your face will go on forever, but when you create a simulation capable of creating a simulation, your whole existence is in that mirror. The sheer number of possible simulated universes would be infinite. If you were living in the real thing, it would be more than exceptional, it would be almost mathematically impossible."

"Almost," said Claire.

"Almost. It's hard to wrap your head around at first, but I guarantee you'll get more frustrated later. When you look around and feel for the first time that you might not be here, it can be liberating. Or overwhelming."

"But that's not science! That's not physics, Marka. Why was Carl studying philosophy and universe chakra crap? That's what I do! Good lord. I'm back where I started."

And Marka was back to where she started as well, patting Claire's knee, still hovering ridiculously close to the floor, but her dry, cracked hand didn't bother Claire anymore.

"We both believed it, at least for a few years. I don't know what I believe now, Claire. But when you're captivated by something, you make your work follow it. What my team is working on now is in imaging. We're capturing visual representations that are impossible to photograph. Images that may offer proof that our reality, our universe, is simulated."

"You're looking for glitches in the matrix?"

"No, we're not looking for faults, we're looking for perfection. Lines that are too straight, rules that can't bend. Nature is not perfect, it's not symmetrical. That would be the sign of a humanoid hand holding the brush."

"It sounds like you're looking for God, Dr. Swandish."

"Maybe *we're* God, Mrs. Méndez."

Claire turned and looked right into Marka's eyes now. Up until this point, she'd been avoiding her face, certain she'd feel hatred for the woman that had stolen Carl's attention decades ago. "If someone is smart enough to build a simulation, wouldn't they be able to cover it up? Make it appear real? Code in the mistakes you think it needs?"

Marka nodded at Claire. "They could. They could. But maybe they want us to find out. Maybe they think we're ready now."

The two aged women talked until past midnight on the floor of the archive room. Eventually they grew tired of waving their arms every 10 minutes to turn the motion-sensor lights back on and made their way back through the server room and to the front door, Claire carrying a cardboard box of Carl's papers. The dark hallway's twinkling lights brought back decades of Christmases and Claire slowed her steps to steep in nostalgia. Marka could feel Claire's reluctance to leave so she guided her toward her small office just to the left of the main entrance. The walls were covered in brilliantly colored pictures, interspersed with unframed, rectangular school portraits of several children.

"The pillars of creation!" boomed Marka as Claire took in the beautiful images. "And these are my creations. Malcolm, Teila and Vicky." Claire looked at her and her throat tightened so that she could barely be heard.

"Why?" she managed, her whole face begging Marka for an explanation she couldn't provide.

"Why what, Claire?"

"Why is everyone named goddamned Vicky?" Claire burst into heaving sobs, taking in too much air and losing her grounding. As she started to fall, Marka squeezed her with a strength that pushed all the air back out, and with it, all the anxiety it held. Time slowed to halt and Claire remembered another lifetime when Carl joked about parallel universes over her rum-sodden breakfast. Claire prayed to Vishnu to transport this moment to one of those places: *don't let her let go. don't let her let go.*

AND IN A VERY CLOSE UNIVERSE, BUT CURLED UP IN A DIMENSION AWAY FROM VIEW, A PRAYER WAS ANSWERED AS IF IT WERE DIRECT COMMAND. MARKA IS STILL HOLDING CLAIRE, MOTIONLESS, SURROUNDED BY STEAMING COFFEE CUPS.

Claire and Marka parted ways and promised to keep in touch.

*

It took Claire a week before she could go through the box from Marka. Armed with a dictionary, a "Physics for Dummies" website and 2 bottles of Chardonnay, she finally tackled some of Carl's papers. She read as much as she could, until the words started to move across the pages in waves, and then concentrated the bulk of her energy on finishing the second bottle.

The second day, she tried again, this time making considerable progress, but always losing her way by the middle third of the paper. She looked through the box again, seeing if something more accessible would make itself known. There was a wad of smaller papers tied together with rubber bands, which Claire unwound out of curiosity. Most of the papers were receipts or carbon copies of equipment orders, but there was also an envelope addressed to Carl at his former lab address:

Dr. Carlos Méndez, Office 32
Challen Hall Physics A
Upper Mississippi University
Minneapolis, MN 55223

The envelope had no return address and showed a postmark from 1979, the year before Claire had walked away. But inside was another, unopened envelope that must have been returned unread:

THE VICKI

Querida Mamá,

I'm writing to you in English because you said you wouldn't talk to me anymore anyway. This is who I am now. I am American and I am proud of my work. I am proud of my family and, yes, I am even proud of Carlos. I know you don't understand him and you don't understand me so I wanted to tell you a story. It's a story about your son and who he really is.

Había una vez

Once upon a time there lived a man named Carlos. He left his papá and mamá in Villa Victoria and didn't look back for a long time. He knew they loved him, but they believed he was going to el infierno and that it was his fault. They said he would burn and bleed if he didn't change. They tried to clean him with agua bendita but he didn't change. They prayed Dios te salve, Maria but he didn't change. And when he went to school and learned Inglés, he definitely didn't change. There he met Manuel. And he no longer wanted to change.

When he moved to America, Mamá and Papá didn't say goodbye. And he never saw them again. One day, he met una mujere named Claire and she made him finally want to change. He loved her more than he loved Manuel or anyone else so he knew it meant that he was changing. After ten years, his mamá picked up the phone. It was too late for her to tell Papá that his son was saved. But she promised to look at his face and walk with him in the streets if he came home. When he came home. But he didn't come home.

The man met another Carlos and this man didn't make him want to change again. He wanted to be the same person he always was, but the other Carlos said he loved him. And the other Carlos said he knew the man better than he knew himself. The man told the other Carlos he was married and had children. That he had changed. He tried to concentrate on his work. But the other Carlos was made of colors and wanted the man to change again.

Mamá would call the other Carlos loco, but he had a blessing called synesthesia. He could hear colors and told the man how they sounded. But the man didn't understand. And because he didn't understand he thought he could keep his life and family, without changing.

But the other Carlos worked very hard to change him back. He worked day and night and built a machine for the man. The machine had tiny fingers that walked over wavelengths of light and made them into sound. The machine translated and amplified everything that was beautiful, like a Victrola. But it was a magic Victrola and he called it the Vicki. And little by little, with la musica de los colores, Carlos made the man change.

When Carlos and Carlos were together, the world looked different and the man was sad and happy and missed his Mamá all at the same time. But she would not pick up the phone again. And so the man never heard la musica of her voice again and had to listen to the Vicki even more. The sounds of the colors got trapped in his head and couldn't get out, filling his mind and his soul. He started to hear the other sounds of the world less, like echoes without their source. His children spoke in black and white and so he started to hear them less than the one who could sing in colors.

The man wants to change again, but this time it's too late. He's listening to the colors and now he can only go toward them.

Te amo mamá
Carlosito

(2010)

Claire muffled the joy of an escaping champagne cork with a dish towel. The release that accompanied the opening had lost its sense of celebration a hundred bottles earlier, but the comfort of the underlying pinot tones would sing her to sleep.

She dreamt of all kinds of men, facing each other as they pulsed together. Claire woke in a hot sweat as she finally knew her husband for the first time. It had been an open secret that Dr. Enders went both ways, but Claire had always thought of his former pairings as experiments, as lust. Claire felt at the same time old and naive as she realized she had never considered two men looking each other in the eyes.

She had to look in the archives at an internet cafe to find news of the funeral; it had been ten years almost to the day and Dr. Enders was no longer big news. But there he was, a black and white photo in the local paper, his hands crossed under his chin. He must have been in his early twenties in the photo. The article was forgivingly brief. Dr. Carl Enders had died in a motorcycle accident at age 53. He was survived by two daughters and was known for his work on simulated universes and color perception theory. A b-grade tabloid photo showed the funeral party, blurred in the rain.

"I didn't know they served wine here," said a chubby woman who sat down next to Claire and took out a set of knitting needles in the middle of the cafe.

"Well, they don't," said Claire with a wink as she pulled a silver plastic bag from her purse, one that must have been extracted from a box of grocery store wine. She proceeded to refill her coffee mug. "A lady needs to take care of herself these days." She looked back at her screen. She pointed at the tall, big man with a cane in the funeral photo. "That's the man who raised my kids," she said for the benefit of her neighbor. But the knitter was concentrated on her mittens and didn't pay Claire any attention.

"It must be him, Carlos. Perhaps he was injured in the accident too." Claire ached as she looked at his grainy image. He had taken care of her girls. She loved him for that. Her grown-up daughters were in the photo too, holding hands. Claire nodded approvingly and wiped a delinquent eye. They'd done just fine without her, just fine.

VISWANATHA
(2010)

They had been separated for the interview and each placed with a government agent. "We're asking the same questions, it's standard procedure."

"Well, your case looks good, very solid. Your sponsor is a retired high-ranking civil servant. Ms. Lambert's recommendation along with your spouse's skilled expertise make this process almost irrelevant. Your citizenship should be granted in the next six months. But I am curious, you said you met at a funeral? I've never heard of that before. How did you know? I mean, how did you know you were meant to be?"

And in two separate rooms, using the vocabularies of their respective generations, Vicky and Suresh tried to explain how they'd heard marimba music raining down from the sky.

II. Saint Kell

KELLERSDORFF-S^T CHARLES §/ ARGENT-LE-NEUF

THE ARBOGASTS

As loyalties swayed from France to Germany and almost tiptoed away from both, the residents of Kellersdorff hid their wine, their jewelry and sometimes whole families in the deep, winding gallery of cellars below their hamlet by the Argent River. They were nearly oblivious to the city of Strasbourg, with its pointed finger of a cathedral rising just two kilometers away, their loyalties lying far down in the *keller*, the hidden network of municipal basements.

Named at some point in its Germanic past for its cellars of unknown origin, Kellersdorff became Saint Charles-sur-Argent during one of several purposeful attempts to Frenchify place names between wars. When German boots pounded through once again the village reclaimed the Kellersdorff appellation for nearly 50 years. By the time the pocket by the river bend went French again, the residents were in agreement that both identities belonged to them, so the area became officially known as Kellersdorff-Saint-Charles-sur-Argent.

A relatively quick burst of German re-occupation and the subsequent return to the Gauls required the town to rise from the charred remains as Kellersdorff-Saint-Charles-sur-Argent-le-Neuf, meaning "the new town on the river." The community's name and history had become so unwieldy that the locals finally resorted to calling their home Saint Kell.

Some said the Arbogasts of St. Kell had descended directly from Mithras, who himself was born from a rock and was forced underground throughout Europe by Christian crusaders. What everyone agreed upon was that the Arbogast name was synonymous with loyalty. The story goes that in 1890 the sprawling Arbogast family of Niedergass was hidden for two years in the cellars of St. Kell while the 200-odd aboveground residents agreed to tell Kaiser Wilhelm's men that the whole offensive family was vacationing in Italy. Apparently, a cohort of brothers calling themselves Arbogasts and accustomed to protection from St. Kell, had snuck into his palace to do an unspecified, but great, disservice to the Prussian's ego during one of his stays in Strasbourg. Rather than identify the offenders, the villagers of St. Kell preferred feigning confusion and claimed to all be named Arbogast.

Strasbourg was evacuated under Nazi pressure in 1939, but most of St. Kell was reluctant to leave, preferring instead to stock their cellars and hunker down. During the occupation in 1940, the mayor of St. Kell held an emergency meeting in the main *keller* below Niedergass and warned of a different kind of hiding. The army would be coming for one of the families in St. Kell, bringing them to the Strasbourg Synagogue. Stories from surrounding villages told him the family would only leave the re-purposed place of worship as smoke. But rather than stowing the family like wine, their fellow residents would hide them in plain view. Everyone from St. Kell was asked to bring their identification documents to the *keller* below. Anything they could find with their names – birth, employment, property and religious documentation – was to be brought down. The mayor's office was temporarily moved underground where teams worked in shifts to produce the new identities. When all was said and done, the people emerged from the *keller*, baptized by the dark with their new names. In October of 1940 all 426 residents of St. Kell bore the name Arbogast. The German army largely ignored the little pocket of St. Kell, and the river Argent kept flowing, determined like the residents were to live as normally as possible in times of turpitude.

By the 1960s, there were still a few Arbogasts left, but most had reclaimed their names from the cellars when the Assembly of Europe set up its headquarters in Strasbourg and convinced both France and Germany that wars were better suited to other regions of the globe. A sweeping planned community, financed by the city of Strasbourg, was to be installed in St. Kell in the early 70s, bringing in detached houses filled with people that were presumably not named Arbogast, and a group of tower blocks for government-subsidized housing.

The new St. Kell would be an urban utopia, modeled after a Bavarian architect's vision of the ideal city, and the whole network of streets bearing artists' names sprang up in three years. Michelagelo, Titian, Goya, Raphael. Colossal villas with broad, landscaped yards reminiscent of American suburbs perched along the Argent. Wealthy hedonists moved in and shamelessly raced their German cars down Niedergass, tearing down to the river to swill Riesling and play absurdly jovial accordion music.

In 1978, Céline and Arnaud Arbogast could hear the parties from the river dwellers blocks away from their home on Niedergass, the street lined with houses from another era and the remains of ancestral farms that now lived to the soundtrack of a loud freeway just behind it. Mamama, Arnaud's thrice-widowed mother and undisputed head of the family, said she'd rather go bury herself in the now bricked-off cellars than leave. "Ich bin Ofira Arbogast von Kellersdorff-Saint-Charles-sur-Argent-le-Neuf. I didn't leave for the Germans and I'm not leaving for a bunch of smelly diesels." And so, the Arbogasts stayed.

For being so close to Strasbourg, St. Kell was cut off from the rest of the city by railroad tracks and nearly encircled by the bend in the river. The ugly towers rising in the backdrop and the climbing degrees of debauchery by the river rich started to make the Arbogasts feel trapped in a no-man's land. After centuries of inertia, the world had changed around them and their one-street old town left them sandwiched between rivaled vices. While the big game hunters and Assembly workers wanted to pickle themselves underground, young and aimless sons of immigrants pushed hash in pastel tracksuits.

The blocks of tower housing rose successively higher and as they reached 15 floors, the view of the villas on the river improved, adding jealousy to the burden of unemployment for the residents of Utopia. They resented the cars, the noise and the lawns. They eventually started to make their own noise and carve out their own identity in St. Kell. A few Molotov cocktails and burnt cars later, the residents of the villas started moving out. Plastic bags now danced across the wide lawns. But the decline of St. Kell didn't reach the notoriety it boasts today until the prison was thrust upon them by the city of Strasbourg, home to the European Assembly and bastion of human rights, in the late 80s. Built behind Niedergass, the St. Kell Prison wall came right up to the property line of Mamama's farmhouse, completing the enclosure for her rabbits.

When his first son, Valéry, was born next to the prison authority's construction cranes, Mamama's son Arnaud announced the family would finally be moving. Maybe they'd even try their hand at New York. He'd heard there was a micro-climate with mineral soil just like home. They could grow Riesling, he reasoned. Let their children thrive like autumn grapes, their one lonely St. Kell vine having been trampled by the prison wall. But as Mamama shook her head slowly, he knew he would never abandon Niedergass while she was alive. And thus Valéry, Nicolas and Marianne Arbogast spent their childhood butted up against the Prison of St.

Kell.

*

(1990)

"*Gottfedoml*" muttered Nico as he once again re-opened the large scab on his right knee by brushing it against the dried wood of his shovel.

"Mamama would kill you if she heard that. And you don't even pronounce it right. Say *Fudegl*. Or better yet, speak French, *Gummizwèrisch*." Calling his little brother a rubber dwarf was a favorite pastime for Valéry, in fact any Alsatian insults made him feel superior since little Nico had trouble with the dialect and spoke only the standard French he learned in *école maternelle*, the neighborhood pre-school.

"Well, *Kässfratz*," piped up Marianne as she called Valéry a cheese-face. The middle child, she had a way with words and had picked up French, Alsatian and a bit of Turkish from St. Kell's Saturday market. "At least he's better at digging than you. We wouldn't have made it this far if it weren't for the little *schnudelnas* and his shovel."

"I'm not a booger-nose," said Nico as he wiped at his face, just to be sure. He put down his shovel and looked at his bleeding knee. After months of digging, cursing and long pauses for *pain au chocolat* in the public tunnels near the river, today would be the day they first heard about the only part of St. Kell they hadn't seen. Mamama Arbogast, their golden-toothed grandmother, boasted that she had travelled to four countries without leaving her home just by being in Alsace, a spot that France and Germany both wanted so much that they took turns protecting it from each other's bombs. But she also talked about the deeper cellar that had been filled in, closed off, walled over and hidden from view for so long that no one believed it was still there, much less accessible.

The municipal cellars of St. Kell had once been connected to several homes on Niedergass and, some said, ran all the way to Strasbourg in an underground network that had since been sealed off to prevent invasions of both rodents and visitors from across the Rhine river. But what most people didn't know was that under the whole network of cellars, there was a deeper, grander cellar that had been around at least as long as the Arbogasts.

*

Marianne's Kinkele, the pet rabbit who had been spared from Mamama's cream sauces, finally passed at the old age of 8 and she was lovingly buried by her brothers in the garden. Their father warned them to dig at least a meter down or the foxes would come for Kinkele. Valéry shoveled dirt around until his arms hurt and the dark set in, then Marianne set the soft, white body in the hole and Nicolas heaped dirt over the top. All three stomped tearfully over the grave, trying their best to make the bunny safe from digging predators, but by morning, the dirt was loose and had a depression in the middle. They couldn't tell if an animal had succeeded in pulling Kinkele out and the thought brought Marianne back to tears. She wanted more than anything to dig again and check, to make the grave deeper, to protect her Kinkele from digging claws and hungry jaws. Mamama pressed Marianne's wet face into her thick apron and stroked her hair. "Kinkele is safe, *Bobele*. If those foxes got to her, they took her to the Unterkeller."

"The Unterkeller?" Nicolas had questioned. None of them had heard that word before. Marianne stopped crying and looked up at Mamama, who was now glancing in the kitchen to see if her son could hear her. Confirming that he couldn't, she crouched down with the trio and started whispering in the mystic tenors that only a heavily-accented grandmother can pull off.

"There are hollows down below. Rabbits like places like that, dark and rounded. Quiet. A deep world for diggers. Kinkele is fine now—she's in the Unterkeller." Arnaud came through the door and Mamama stood up while brushing off her skirt. The children sensed that this was a secret between themselves and their grandmother, so they only questioned her when their parents were out of earshot. Mamama relished in their curiosity and tried her best to make her replies cryptic.

Mamama revealed how she used to get to the Unterkeller, which was now probably right below the prison. She'd go through a door in the rabbit shed, which led to the neighbor's barn and then across to a small wooden trap door in the floor that was covered with hay. She'd go down to the cellar and cross back over to the other side, now a level below her own rabbits. She would find a small opening in the corner and take the long, uneven stairs that wound down another two stories to the Unterkeller. There was a great rectangular room, she'd said, with arched ceilings and stone benches along the sides. *Unconventional things happened in unconventional rooms*, she added.

When the young Arbogasts took on the task of finding the elusive Unterkeller, they knew it wouldn't be easy. But they had a whole summer ahead of them before the *rentrée* and going from the prison wall of St. Kell to the prison of their desks. Nico would have to finally learn to read this year and Valéry would be layered with homework while Marianne would take up her tedious piano lessons again. They knew this was their only opportunity. So the intrepid trio had spit on their dirty hands and shaken in agreement that they would find the cave before the end of summer.

The foundations of the St. Kell Prison went deep—too deep, it seemed, to allow any suspicious digging in the area by three ragged siblings with shovels. They'd tried Mamama's route and encountered poured concrete and cinderblock walls where the stairwell should have been. But their curiosity and Mamama's flashing gold smile told them there was another point of access for the finding.

Valéry gave Mamama an extra glass of schnapps after dinner all week in hopes of teasing out clues, but she'd usually just start singing *"du kom di missilë"* for him, ending with "ding, ding" and a nose tweak. It was a song about a mouse crawling up and down, ringing various bells, but Valéry didn't seem amused.

"Really, Mamama, is there another way?" he'd press.

"Come here, Bobele." Everyone under the age of 40 was a *bobele*, a baby, to Mamama. "Don't tell your papa, but I'm sure you could get in there, little *missele*, my tiny mice. You could go through the big game hunter's house on Raphaelgasse, sneak right in like rodents. Oh, *fudegel.* They had so many parties over there; they must have had quite a wine cellar. I remember walking by when they were building that place. They had machines helping them, something the old town never had. They were digging pretty deep. There could be as much of that house below as there is above."

*

The two story white house was ridiculously grand, even for the newer part of St. Kell. It sat on *rue* Raphael, the real name of the street that Mamama insisted on calling Raphaelgasse in her native tongue. A round tower with a pointed, shingled roof looked like a cross between a witch's hat and a chateau. Over-sized picture windows were covered in vines and wooden roll-down shutters. Two-men-high rose bushes dangled pink blooms over a barely visible path that was choked with weeds. Grass was growing out of the cracks in the thick stone steps.

Valéry led the group over the fence into an unkempt backyard. Dead leaves and pine needles made a thick carpet over the ground. Rusty gardening tools rested against the house, sharing their orange oxidation with the house's white paint. Blackened, moldy walnuts crushed under their feet as they circled the house looking for a way in.

"Schnudelnas, do you think you can fit through there?" asked Valéry of his little brother as he pointed to a small rectangular flap on the side of a glassed-in porch. It was a dog door, locked shut with a metal latch that gave after two kicks from Val sent it swinging on its hinges. Nicolas didn't respond until after he had squirmed sideways through the door and sprung up on the other side of the glass in a Peter Pan stance.

"I'm not a *schnudelnas*!" he shouted through the yellowed pane and then pulled his pants down to show holey grey underwear to his siblings before running off giggling into the house. Marianne banged on the glass and pleaded with Nicolas to open the door, but was afraid of raising her voice since the house next door was still inhabited. She turned around nervously to see if any neighbors were getting too curious then turned her attention back to the dark house her brother had disappeared into.

"Bear! There's a bear!" came a high-pitched voice from inside. Nico came bounding back out to the porch with excitement. "Marianne, there's a bear inside. He's a hundred times bigger than Doudours. Come look." He fiddled around and turned a key that was graciously left behind on the other side of the door, letting his sister in. Valéry followed behind.

They walked gingerly around giant ghosts— massive pieces of carved furniture covered in flowered sheets—and swept sticky cobwebs aside. Sure enough, in the first room they found an upright taxidermied bear with a strand of dusty Christmas lights strung around its neck. It was indeed bigger than Doudours, Nico's teddy bear and confidant. The walls were lined with different heads: boar, deer, elk and moose, some sporting limp Santa hats. Interspersed with the mounted animals were blank spaces displaying yellowed outlines of plaques on the wall where some other unfortunate creatures had previously been attached. The door to a central hallway was propped open with a strangely-shaped mass that appeared to be an elephant's foot.

Light filtered into the round tower room through slats in the shutters, clearly showing the outline of two boys. Nico ran up to them, seeing up close that they were bronze varieties of himself, two boys older than toddlers, but not yet showing wisdom in their round metal cheeks. "I want!" came his familiar refrain as Nico tried to lift one who was holding bronze grapes. He strained until his face flushed crimson and the statue levitated a millimeter off the ground.

"You'll get hurt, put that down," said Marianne as she stroked the cold cheek. "He is cute though. Looks a bit like you, Nico." Nicolas smiled and dropped the boy the short distance to the floor with a dull thud, then wrapped his arm around the motionless boy's shoulders. Twins.

"We need to get down lower. Let's find the basement," came the commanding big brother wisdom of Valéry. The three returned to poking around, opening doors to messes of cobwebs and endless furniture. Finally, Valéry's voice came again, from farther away this time. "This way, there are stairs. Come on." Marianne took Nico's hand and ducked under more webs toward the sound of his voice. A wooden door waited ahead, open a few feet, but showing only darkness on the other side. Nicolas tugged at Marianne's arm with increasing force, willing her to continue and taunting her for being afraid of the dark. A skinny beam of light finally angled out the wood frame accompanied by Valéry's voice. "I brought a light, Marianne. Do we have Schnudelnas?" A resounding thud as Val was knocked to the ground by a boy half his age confirmed that they did.

The three pressed on, accompanied by the fine beam of light and intermittent sneezes. "The air isn't the same here," explained Marianne as she covered her face again to expel. "It's almost too old to breathe," she complained as they forged ahead, low and slow in air that was suspiciously warmer than the cellar's just meters away. Her fear of small spaces tended to manifest in the form of breathing troubles. The dark and the dank competed to be fearsome, transforming the staleness into a mounting heat as the trio turned corners. Its invasion into local lungs dragged the explorers with purpose and sent them teetering to the brink of panic and claustrophobia as they continued with outstretched arms.

Seven minutes later, which felt more like seventy, glowing stripes of light shone through a slatted door at the end of the tunnel. Valéry approached the door and peered through the slats. A small, square room with fake wood paneling was visible in the un-natural underground light. Carpets covered the floor, heaping in some places to several layers thick. A boy and a man sat in a corner, motionless.

Marianne and Nico crowded up next to Valéry to stare, undetected, at the pair. Nico sniffed his runny nose and the boy in the room looked up as if he'd heard. "Be quiet, Schnudelnaus!" said Valéry, but it was his harsh whisper, not the sniffling, that betrayed their presence. The man in the room looked directly at the door and stood up. He walked over the wooden door and pushed it open with all his strength, dragging the bottom across the dirt floor of the tunnel and pushing the Arbogasts back.

The man saw the three terrified children and smiled broadly. "*As-Salaam-Alaikum*! I've never seen anyone come in this way before. Welcome!"

"Where are we?" asked Nico, still standing in the passage, but now bathed in light.

"Oh, you don't know? Then the grace of Allah brought you here." said the man. He had a scruffy beard and gentle face. "You're at 32 Grünewald. This is where we talk to our souls. You are welcome to stay and get to know yours."

Valéry looked to his sister who was shivering, not with cold, but fear. He knew the claustrophobia had gotten the better of her and that she wouldn't last much longer underground. He couldn't make her go back through the dark tunnel again. "Monsieur," started Valéry, but he was interrupted by the man.

"You can call me Halit. And this is my son, Mehmet."

Only now did Marianne pipe up weakly in response to the man's initial greeting. "*Wa-Alaikum As-Salaam.*" She'd heard it a thousand times at the market and was happy to finally repeat it underground, away from her Maman's ears.

"Halit" continued Valéry, "can you show us an easier way out of here?"

Halit nodded and then motioned with his head. "This way, little explorers."

They turned a corner, walked up a surprisingly few stairs and came out into the bright gray daylight of St. Kell through a green door at the base of a tower block building. "Do you live in the Painter's Quarter? Can you get home?" Valéry replied that they were from the old town, but that he could find his way back. Just as they were leaving, Halit placed one hand on top of Nico's head and the other on Mehmet's. "Same size, you two. Will you be going to school this year too, little one? Nico nodded, making Halit's hand bob up and down. "Good," said Halit. "So we'll see you at the *rentrée*."

THE ASSEMBLY
(2000)

Curious. Courteous. Ambitious. Something about Nils Winter made him leave impressions on people that were one word long. As former Prime Minister of Sweden and soldier for democracy, there was one word used to describe his re-election as Secretary General of the Assembly of Europe: Unanimous. Mr. Winter had first taken office almost ten years ago and had since built his reputation as the authority on prisoner well-being in greater Europe. He had become an expert at knowing precisely what to laud and what to condemn in front of multilingual media firms. The Secretary General lauded measures, but condemned actions. He lauded stances and condemned remarks. He lauded motions and condemned attacks. But after years brandishing his secular human values, he found that his flag manager, Marten, was lowering various member colors more frequently than usual. Whether terror attacks or wars with muddied meaning, the dropping flags were commemorating some shared sense of suffering on the part of Nils from his cream-carpeted office in Strasbourg just over the main awning that leaked when it rained. He sensed that the world was changing, that he was poised at the edge of an incomprehensible cliff, conscious of the fact that the balance would indeed shift toward more condemnations in the future.

His final term was winding down, and along with it a life of service for the Continent. Nils was going through the motions of closing his political career, but couldn't help but focus on what was ahead, his plans to finally make a real mark on his world, to work his way through all the mysteries Aunt Vicky had told him about as a child. He would do it here, in the city that had cradled him for a decade, forgetting his stumbles into ego politics and cold canals after lovers' spats. He was thankful for Strasbourg, the city whose medieval walls had soaked in all his secrets, without letting escape a

71

word of Serbian mistresses or bad judgment regarding visiting Belorussian teacher trainers.

His wife, Hannah, wore blue eyeliner well into her sixties and kept her bobbed pale hair as springy as her step. A sporadic handful of daisies was enough for his lifelong companion, but the women of the Assembly expected perfume and signatures for their pet projects. Nils knew Hannah would never leave him, but her naiveté was on display in her interpretation of his need for variety in the bedroom. She dutifully switched sides of the bed each night, her head set on shaking up the routine a she dozed off at 9 pm sharp. Nils continued to sign documents deep into the perfumed wee hours.

The only time Nils had considered leaving Hannah for more than a night at a time was when he'd met a beautiful Latvian Deputy at an environmental awareness reception. He went on a fact-finding mission in her Latvian wetlands and became convinced that they shared priorities. Nils got the essentials on paper, that Ms. Svototska's environmental program did indeed fall under the scope of acceptable democratic initiatives, and determined that his feeling of constant falling was both a fine appetite suppressant and a mind-altering drug. Nils Winter was at his best when he was hopelessly in love.

But he stayed with Hannah as she anchored him to a life of service. His only protest movement was his wardrobe of blue suits. No matter how many times Marten the social secretary would have invitations printed with "smart casual" or "garden fare" people inevitably showed up in black suits and black dresses. Nils sipped champagne happily even as Hannah said he was dressed like a TV mailman.

Nils displayed a sepia portrait of a close-eyed Winston Churchill behind his desk. He was sure it projected the sort of meditative humility that a Secretary General should espouse. It tended to make visitors opposite the desk perform the stiff facial contortions of someone trying not to visibly yawn.

The Assembly's lofty core values of Peace, Justice and Solidarity were eclipsed at the individual employees' level by resume-padding, networking and income tax avoidance. In Strasbourg, the Assembly of Europe felt bustling and important, distinguished and pristine. But outside of the Alsace region, most people hadn't heard of the international organization that counted 47 member countries and mowed through endless budget requests for projects and programs that somehow tied far-flung topics of personal interest into study visits on liberty. Even within Strasbourg, the Assembly was blurred in most minds with the other European institutions that shared a campus and a corps of interpreters. The European Union headquarters were just across the river and connected by a bustling eurocrat bridge.

But Nils had successfully negotiated two prizes for Strasbourg over his terms at the Assembly. The first was an enormous jailhouse, which moved all the detainees from St Marguerite, a prison in the city center, downstream to St. Kell, a decaying bend in the Argent River. The now-empty St Marg, just upriver from its former inmates, was prime real estate. Nils worked behind the scenes for months with his French Ambassador, Jacqueline Cheval, in order to finagle another great move. *L'Ecole Nationale d'Administration*, the Paris elitist institution that groomed French politicians and journalists, moved to the now empty jail in Strasbourg under his watch. Strasbourg would remain on the map by churning out diplomats. Nils and Jacqueline took the opportunity to reflect on the genius of preemptively sending the Paris politicians to prison, while giving the hardened inmates of St. Kell new digs. An experimental human rights program would take place at St. Kell Prison, insuring that Nils would have another purpose in Strasbourg when his second term was up.

Nils was often lost in his giant cubic home, but the size of the paintings (and their hair trigger alarms) gave him a continuous sense of importance. Earlier inhabitants had complained about the traffic due to the proximity of Place de la République, but Nils found his large private garden a quaint and aging paradise, just steps from Strasbourg's busiest tram station, with its passers-through and all their plebeian dialogue clearly heard through the high hedge. Unfortunately, his wife had continuous issues with the electricity and found that her high heels sunk too deeply into the lawn. Nils feigned a shared sense of misery, but adored his surroundings and lobbied for renovation, when necessary, rather than relocation.

He also truly appreciated his staff, which included a tall and jovial gate opener/shoulder massager/caterer named Marten and a girlfriend of said employee with unnaturally white teeth. The young couple brought sense back to the world for Nils and he liked nothing more than to sit with them on the back balcony, exploring the low-class realms of movies and TV. Marten poured a mean French 75 and his cheery tan companion with her long floral dresses and chubby cheeks could chat the angst out of any afternoon.

THE ARGENTORATUM
(1990)

Neither Valéry nor Marianne wanted to make another trip underground after finding the basement mosque, but finding that he was more efficient by himself, Nico knew his exploration had just begun. He no longer prodded his siblings to go exploring. He'd set off on his own a few more times, repeating the same trail underground, starting with his metal likeness on rue Raphael each time. But looking at the nearly identical bronze boys the fourth time, Nico had realized who he needed as an underground companion — someone just his size. When school started in September, Nico arrived first in his grade and trained his eyes on the classroom entrance, hoping his future partner in crime would soon come through the door. He started to lose hope as grandmothers and parents dropped off child after child, some clinging more than others, but none recognizable to Nico.

The teacher had already started doing introductions when Nico heard cries approaching from the hallway. Gripped onto a black-veiled woman's leg was Mehmet, tears streaming down his pink face and dampening the dark curls that framed it. Nico pulled out the tiny wooden chair next to him, but Mehmet didn't notice through his sobbing. When Nicolas stood up and walked over to the boy the teacher stopped and the class quieted. He grabbed the boy's hand and pulled him over to the little chair next to him. He said in a loud voice to the whole class, "I'm Nico and this is my friend, Mehmet." A chorus of *bonjours* echoes around the room.

"Mo." came Mehmet's voice, drawing on the strength of Nico's. "You can call me Mo." He sniffled loudly once, but never cried at school again.

With Nico's father working a second job and his mother eternally stationed in front of her stove, Nico was free to wander. He went to Mo's cramped apartment on the eleventh floor and kicked around Mo's room until his father sent them to air out in the utopian garden, which consisted of a broken swing-set and a graffitied climbing structure surrounded by burnt wooden benches. Mo's mother cleaned offices in Strasbourg so Nico never saw her after that first day of school. The boys would run out and play 'wolf' then 'color wolf' before sneaking through the green door, across the carpets and into the underground maze.

*

(1994)

By the time they were ten, they continued to stop by the basement mosque, but where Nico grew more interested in the dominant religion of the painters' quarter, Mo drifted inconspicuously away from it. Nico always wanted to know more about Mohammed, Mehmet's eponym, but Mo was bored by all of it. His own family was attending prayers less and less. When Nico decided to fast for Ramadan, he was appalled to find Mo eating Malteasers in his bunk bed. If he could no longer interest Mo in reading the Koran in the basement, he knew another yarn, borrowed from his grandmother would draw him back underground. He gave a first-person narrative, as if his Mamama herself were sitting on a pile of carpets two stories below the street.

> My father, your great grandfather, wasn't some sort of revolutionary, but he was a prankster. He saw Kaiser Wilhelm roll into town every few months in a fancy Mercedes and he could see in the faces of everyone he drove by what it did to them. The Kaiser was trying to make everybody build another wall around Strasbourg, but none of the locals would do it. He'd come check the progress every now and then and try to make the people forget their French. Forget their food. Eat more sauerkraut. He changed all the names of buildings and his dad built him a palace.

> My father followed that ugly parade around town and watched where he parked that car, in a building with stone horse heads sticking out the sides. He knew the tunnels below the city like the back of his hand. Wilhelm never even knew there were so many mice crawling underneath his palace. He sure didn't know when my daddy tunneled in right below his stable to steal his mechanical horse, the fanciest car of his time.

> He drove it underground all the way to St. Kell and that's where he met my mother. They hid the car in the Unterkeller and it's still down there today.

Mo interrupted at this point. "That doesn't make any sense, he couldn't drive the car underground. None of the tunnels are big enough. And how would he get into the stable in the first place? A Kaiser? Isn't that like a king or something? He would have better security than that. And-"

"Okay, okay. So he probably drove it above ground and parked it in the barn or something. But it is true. I'm sure it's true. She's told me this story a hundred times. She says the car is in St. Kell. A 1915 Mercedes. It's been there since before she was born and no one else knows about it."

If Mo had been one year older, he probably wouldn't have gone for it, but the prospect of the old car did intrigue him. He pressed on, "Why wouldn't she tell anybody about it? Why not sell it? That has to be worth a fortune."
Nico trusted Mo enough to tell him. "She says no one can find out because her dad was a criminal. That makes our whole family criminals. She was so scared that someone would find out who her dad was. When everyone in St. Kell had the opportunity to became Arbogasts for a year, Mamama finally let her guard down. She changed her name from Lanvin to Arbogast and lost all trace of her car thief father in her name. It wasn't just that Hebrew family we were saving by going Arbogast. So we can't change our names back, there's still a warrant out for Lanvin."

*

"You don't have to hurt everyone, Nico. You don't have to keep defending me," said Mo as his friend pulled him to standing after a scuffle with a neighbor. But Nico persistently sought out occasions to beat people up. Since Mo was looking less and less like his neighbors from St. Kell, with his penchant for collared, ironed shirts, Nico had ample opportunity. The thrill of the punch felt just like falling, the contact of the bones with a bit of flesh between them. He needed it, like he'd needed to bite the bathtub and break his tooth, like he'd needed to ride his bike straight down a ravine, like he'd pin himself under a tree branch in the water to test his lungs. Mo could never understand how Nico's teeth ground at night and his feet bounced imperceptibly all day, vibrating his desk with the whir from below.

As they walked away from the scene of the fight, Mo felt he owed Nico some long-lost enthusiasm for the netherworld and came up with the brilliant plan of following the electrical cords that snaked along the ceiling of the makeshift mosque and out into the tunnels. They'd surely find something this way. The cloth-wrapped cord guided them through several turns of the corridor and back above ground inside a utility shed. They could see out of a broken window that they were housed in a stucco salmon-colored building that they had accessed via a spiral metal stairwell. The building was one open room with a thick coat of dust and leaves on the floor and several additional broken windows. Two metal doors on opposite ends did not yield. The only way forward was down one of the other three identical stairwells that dipped into darkness in the high-ceilinged room.

The first and second stairwell went only six steps down before a metal grate blocked the stairs. The other side was densely packed dirt that filled the entire space of the passage and seeped through the grate to a heap on the other side as well. Nico was delighted to find the last stairwell open and flicked his flashlight back on. Mo cautiously followed. The stairs were a metal spiral again, this time twisting lower and lower until they gave way to stone carved steps at the very bottom. A thick twisted bunch of cords was following the top of the tunnel walls this time.

The walls of the tunnel, which had started as the dirt and rock held back by metal mesh, transformed after few minutes of walking into fully bricked walls with perfectly rounded ceilings. The boys' flashlights revealed electric bulbs every few meters at the height of the cables, but the only light they gave was a dull reflection from their dusty surfaces as the flashlights trained on them.

The brick hallway seemed to branch off in several directions, but most were walled off after a few meters in the same way the access by Mamama's was. Cinder blocks filled the passage from the floor up, with cement filling in the gap between the top row and the arched ceiling. Someone had clearly opted against accessibility.

Above-ground Nico and Mo had little left in common except for their black fingernails, which Mo clacked on the dried ivories of his piano as Nico paged through the Koran in preparation for the opening of a new mosque in St. Kell. Mo's father wanted to ensure his son's escape from what he called *ce banlieu pourri*, this rotten suburb, by getting him a German tutor and a chess coach. But the boys were the same down below the surface. The darkness hid the combed, carefully shaped hair on Mo's head and the accumulation of scars from Nico's battles with gravity.

They rounded a last corner and the passage opened into a wide room with stone benches running along its sides. The floor rose up to meet the ceiling in a full arch.

"You know what this is, don't you, Nico?"

"A party room?" As he looked at their new discovery, he realized that he was standing in the Unterkeller that Mamama had whispered about years before.

"Nico, it's a mithraeum. Remember, from the museum?" His voice sounded strangely rehearsed, as though he'd been planning this discovery for some time.

Nico had stood outside and smoked for most of the field trip to the Strasbourg Historical Museum, so he had nothing to reply.

"They found one of these across the river in Koenigshoffen, but everything had been smashed by the Christians. This one is completely intact. I wonder where the tauroctony is. Nico, look for a bull."

Nico's puzzled look made Mo continue his lesson in the shadows. It was becoming clear that Mo had found the mithraeum before and now recited a well-planned lecture.

"Mithraism was a really old religion. So old that no one knows much about it. But they've found caves like these all over the place. They're temples. And they always have this weird scene in them—a statue or a carving of Mithras slaying a bull—the tauroctony. There are other animals too, but I don't remember what they are. There definitely should be a bull though. Let's find it and I'll show you." But as the boys ran their hands around all the walls and traced both floor and ceiling with flickering flashlight beams, they found no such statue. Nico wouldn't lay eyes on Mithras until that evening, when he looked him up in Marianne's encyclopedia and planted a seed of obsession.

For the next month, the distance between them closed back up. Mo drew Nico back into the mystery. They were whole again in their secret society underground. They called the society of two the Argentoratum and it met weekly, inventing potions and chanting chants, as if its very goal was infusing every action with meaning. They brought camping lanterns and started decorating. Nico knew that Mo liked all the tessellating patterns in the tiles of the new mosque being built so he made sure to stop by the building site and help himself each morning. By the time the builders noticed their shrinking supply of wall covering, Nico had tiled one full wall of the mithraeum.

The Argentoratum let conversation flow uninterrupted and became a sort of underground confessional. Something about the dim light and barely distinguishable echo let the pair reveal much more than at street level. Mo talked about all the girls he liked, each week seemingly enamored anew. He even admitted to experimenting with the baker's daughter, a round girl with discernable acne, and her even rounder cousin. Nico confessed to squeezing his sister's rabbit too hard as a child and presented a correlation between the timing of his father's missing watch and his first purchase of hashish.

Nico contemplated Mo, writing something in his journal and backdropped by tessellating stars. A whisper of an idea came to mind, that he should keep his friend here and refuse to let him resurface, making sure he'd never quit the Argentoratum. He still wondered if it was chance that had led the pair there or if Mo knew something more than him about the mithraeum. Something told him Mo would soon leave him. A thousand thoughts ran through his head in a split second, thoughts of captives and prey, requiring a physical shake to tamp them down.

"I didn't say anything, Nico. Why are you shaking your head?"

*

"Nico, I'm changing schools. My dad got me into the European Academy."

"You're going to Strasbourg?"

"St. Kell is part of Strasbourg, dummy."

"You know what I mean. You're going to be with all those Assembly snots on the north side. When do you start?" He tried to seem nonchalant, but he knew what it meant. Mo was leaving him behind and the Argentoratum would have a membership roster of one.

Mo said he'd start the following term. "Next term is next week. Are you even coming to paint the tunnel? It's your design, Mo." The whole class was supposed to participate in the project to beautify a drug trafficking zone, an above-ground tunnel that linked the Painters' Quarter to the junior high.

"Well, it's during school hours at the Academy. I can't miss class the first week of the term. My dad says there was a waiting list."

"So, no then. Do you think I'm going to paint those stupid teeth if you're not there?" Nicolas had found Mo's sketch of the project childish, one end displaying a giant open mouth and the other a rainbow, but he'd never insulted it until now.

"Nico, I'll still see you after school. It's not like I'm moving."

"Well, don't join the debate team or anything," Nico returned.

"My dad actually signed me up for the chess club."

Both boys burst out laughing as they realized Mo was turning into everything they'd previously mocked about the kids who commuted to school from St. Kell, wearing suits on the tram.

*

(2000)

Mo trickled out of Nico's life as he spent more and more time with his new friends, friends whose parents worked at the Assembly and drove big cars. Eventually his family packed up their grubby apartment and moved north, where the houses were packed together, but the neighborhood was free from what Mo's dad called *la racaille*. Mo stopped by Niedergass on his way out of town, knocking on the door of the Arbogast home, but found only Mamama at home. Mo tried to speak French with her, but Mamama's golden smile only pumped out Alsatian as she handed him cookies and patted his shoulders.

"This is my address, for Nico if he ever wants to come over. He needs to take 2 buses, but it's not too far." He gave Ofira Arbogast the paper and thanked her for the cookies as he left and joined his parents for their long-awaited departure from St. Kell. Mamama nodded and closed the door.

*

(2002)

Two years went by, both full and fast. Mo interned at the Assembly and alternated mock UN meetings with rugby. It was his final year of school and he'd soon be taking the *baccalaureat* leaving exam and applying for universities. He was surrounded by piles of books on his bed when his dad came to say he had a visitor.

Mo came down to the kitchen and saw the familiar face of Marianne. Nico's sister was three years their senior and had always been tall, but Mo had

81

almost caught up and could look at her from a different angle now. Her hair was lighter and longer than he remembered, but she still looked like a prettier version of Nico.

"Mamama gave me your address. Nico's been missing for three days. I know it's been awhile, but…" She trailed off as she looked around at the gleaming kitchen appliances, realizing she'd made a mistake in coming. Mo's family didn't have a shred in common with hers anymore.

"Marianne, it's been two years. I'm glad you came; it's so good to see you, it really is. But you should ask one of Nico's friends. I haven't seen him once since we moved."

Marianne nodded and visibly swallowed before her voice started coming out too fast. "It's just that Nico doesn't have any friends, none that I know of anyway. He's just by himself all the time. He goes away sometimes and I know he likes to walk by the river, but like I said, it's been three days and I don't know if he's okay or if he's left or if he's mad at me or-" She finally stopped for a full breath. "Mo, do you know where he could have gone?"

Mo pointed straight down. "Downstairs?" asked Marianne, perplexed.

"Lower," he replied. "I'm sorry but your brother has become somewhat of a mole. Come on, I'll help you find him. Oh, I'm going by my full name again, Marianne." As he donned a wool coat and cashmere scarf, Marianne's heart raced as she saw her little former neighbor in a new light. Mehmet had become painfully handsome.

When Mehmet offered his arm to Marianne as she climbed off the second bus, she suddenly felt shame for her neighborhood. Their homecoming was met by young men in outfits called joggings, sport attire for the athletics of cigarette tossing and popping gas-powered wheelies along the main pedestrian street. One cigarette grazed Mehmet's cashmere coat. A short, scrubby kid with beige teeth came right up to him and spoke inches from his face. "*Tu reviens au bled,* Mo-Mo?"

"No, I'm not back. I'm just helping Marianne find her brother," said Mehmet without slowing his long paces."

"Nicolas? If that weirdo's alive, he's at the abandoned house on Raphael, *Inch'Allah.*"

They thanked the kid and kept moving. Mehmet saw Marianne as the frog who'd been sitting in the water as it slowly heated to a boil, whereas he had been thrown in. He was astonished by the toll two years had taken on the main square, which was now lined with dark, cracked glass windowfronts and graffitied metal shutters. All the shops had closed, save a vegetable market with overripe, half-priced produce and an old bakery filled with cheap Chinese toys where the croissants should have been. He wanted to leap back out of the boiling water, but knew he had to help find his former friend.

Marianne and Mehmet left the square, but turned toward the tower blocks of the painters' quarter instead of continuing to the house by the river. Mehmet brought them to a green, wooden door at the base of his old apartment building. Marianne was surprised that the door was unlocked and followed the grown-up boy into the basement of the building. The room looked familiar somehow, but as she fought to remember, Mehmet told her this used to be the mosque.

"In a basement? Why?"

"This was the only space we had. There was always water leaking in. And rats. Eventually, they built a new one, a real one with tiles. Kind of a wimpy minaret though," he said with a half-laugh. The Catholics and Muslims of St. Kell had tugged the dimensions up and down until they'd settled on a spire that poked just above the tree line. "I never even made it inside," added Mehmet. He and his family hadn't practiced their faith as enthusiastically as their neighbors and were even labeled apostates by some of the herd.

As they continued through the room, its sheets of faux-wood paneling curving up away from the walls with moisture, another door became visible and a familiar sense of unease came back. As they walked through the other side into the darkness, Marianne felt the strangle of panic come back. She now remembered when she'd been here before. It was the first time she'd seen little Mo, legs crossed in the corner, and now here he was by her side in the tunnel.

"I—I can't," she said in the suffocating space. They had rounded a corner with enough light to see that there was no visible end to the tunnel. "I can't see the way out."

"Close your eyes, Marianne," he said patiently. He stood behind her and put both arms around her, crossing in front of her shoulders. The confinement of Mehmet's arms and the darkness of her closed eyes somehow made her feel less enclosed.

"We need to keep going. He has to be down here." Slowly at first, then picking up speed, Marianne kept moving with Mehmet directing her from behind. He didn't loosen his grip around her shoulders, but just kept willing her on in the dark, not unhappy to tuck his head closer to hers as their feet plodded forward. They made it all the way to the spiral stairs into the salmon-colored building before she blinked open her eyes. He left a space between the two of them now and her back felt cold where he had pressed his body. He started to lead her to the other stairwell, but Marianne protested, "No, not back down, Mehmet. Please." Seeing the genuine terror in her eyes, he nodded and they agreed that he would go look for Nico alone and she would wait in the stairwell room, reassured by the natural light that entered through broken windows. But when he started down the other stairwell, a tighter panic arose in Marianne's chest than before. Quickly weighing which of the two situations was worse, she ran to the stairwell and joined Mehmet in the dark again. This time, she pressed into him and placed his arms in the same position as before, but held on to them on her chest. She decided that not only could she go on with him, but that she even preferred his warmth underground to his distance above.

"Marianne," whispered Mehmet as their steps came to a stop in the tunnel. "Open your eyes."

A pale blue light was coming from around a corner and the air felt significantly warmer. Marianne's curiosity overtook her fear and she pulled away, moving toward the source of light. They both turned another corner and found themselves in a grand room with an arched ceiling and a tiled wall. The surprise registered on Mehmet's face even more than Marianne's.

"It didn't look like this before," he said quietly, but his words were drowned out by the hum of the great machine before them. Mehmet ran his hand along the smooth top of it, a shoulder-height metal box with hundreds of tiny blue lights intermittently flicking on and off at random intervals. It made the air look like the trail of a sparkler that never went out. He looked at Marianne. They'd been reunited for exactly two hours and had barely known one another in the past, but the blue light invited him to kiss her and she gave every bit right back.

"Mo!" came a voice from the other side of the machine, startling the pair apart. Nico appeared, bathed in the same mottled blue like a second Marianne. "You're back, Mo! You've come to bring the bull back. The mithraeum could never be complete without it. And you brought my sister, you devil." His hair was savage and his shirt streaked with something dark. Mehmet offered his hand and Nico took it in a vigorous shake, pumping up and down until he suddenly stopped, Mehmet's hand still in his.

"You haven't come to return the tauroctony." He turned wide-eyed toward his sister.

"I don't understand, Nico," she said sadly, finally seeing the madness people saw in her brother that she had tried so long not to acknowledge.

"But you do, Marianne. He's a thief. He stole the American and now he's trying to steal you."

THE AMBASSADOR
(2000)

Nils Winter had planted the book on a dark oak coffee table next to a dark oak paneled wall eight months prior. Marten had to dust it off from time to time between soirées as it tended to gather dust more profusely than any other object in the dark oak room with the dark oak floor. Maybe it had to do with the glossy technicolor cover, a magnet for stray particles in the air. Something had changed in Nils when he first saw the pictures from that book, their larger versions on display as part of a traveling exhibition from Bremen called "Frontiers of Chaos." Each picture spoke a thousand words echoed from the bedtime stories of Aunt Vicky. He'd purchased the coffee table book a year ago and walked away with a piercing desire to understand his surroundings.

This evening was another opportunity for his wife to light copious quantities of candles and for Marten the chef/butler/book wiper to charm the guests with lightly smoked salmon and green pea purée. The dessert would be raspberries and chocolate or chocolate with raspberries, depending on Nils' mood. There would be singing, hopefully only the pretty Azeri Permanent Representative and not the Czech Ambassador, but you never really knew, did you? The Irish office assistant who always wormed his way onto the guest list would throw back soft cheeses and champagne while playing piano at steadily increasing volumes. Still, Nils held out hope that a partner for his venture would make him or herself known at his last official reception.

The Secretary General told a few holiday jokes from his mount on the stairwell, trying with all his being not to mention Christmas, his favorite holiday, as the institution he represented was firmly secular. The ringing bells and foie gras canapés were for the New Year. Or snow. Or something.

Nils Winter raised a glass and tried to connect human rights to meatballs with lingonberries, then paused for light applause. His speechwriter's contract didn't include social events and after two 5-year terms, fresh material was as hard to come by as a non-navy blue suit in his wardrobe.

The night was winding down as fur coats and small talk started to swish through the grandiose doors into the cold night. Marten the doorman/dishwasher/fire marshal had been let off early to celebrate 1 year of cohabitation with his delightful American companion, with whom he'd verified the candles and their proximity to flammable secular wreaths before retiring to his suite above the garage. Nils took his post near the cloakroom and went through the motions of initial goodbyes with the stream of darkly-clad diplomats who had served him in Strasbourg. When the last spouses had sufficiently commented on Mr. Winter's eye for photography and his wife's avant-garde taste in coral statues, Nils removed his shoes and walked back into his favorite dark oak room. There sat Andrei Soltanovsky, the Russian Ambassador, engrossed in the book on the dark oak table, his feet lightly bouncing on the dark oak floor.

"Andrei," said Nils, not the least bit disappointed that a straggler had remained, "my friend with the deep holes." He was referring to the Kola Superdeep bore hole project, meant to drill through the earth's crust. Andrei and Nils had met a few years back at the celebration party when the drill had reached 12,000 meters in Andrei's Russian hometown in the fringe country of the Assembly's reach. Nils had felt optimistic about Andrei ever since, due to his apparent love of exploring the unknown. "How goes the drilling, my friend?"

Andrei didn't take his eyes off the book, but responded. "It's been twenty years now that we've been drilling, Mr. Secretary. Imagine our Earth is an apple. We haven't even broken through the skin yet."

"But you will soon, my friend," said Nils. "You will indeed."

Andrei looked up from the book. "You know, Sir, it's hotter than we'd ever imagined down there. And yes, it is a very deep hole, but if we go much farther our drills will start to melt." He took a long pause while his buffed nails stroked the spine of the book in his hand and then continued. "We must be careful about things that prefer to remain hidden underground, Mr. Secretary. My son in-law was an engineer at Kola. He killed himself when they got too deep. Said he heard screams from hell down there."

Nils remembered the condolence book he'd signed last year and made the connection to Andrei. He risked dumping the wrong name for the deceased to win over Andrei's trust. "But I thought Boris died in the hospital," he replied.

"He drank 2 liters of vodka, Sir. Even in Russia, we call that suicide."

Andrei realized he was making his de facto boss uncomfortable and brought his attention back to the book. "What am I looking at here, Mr. Secretary?"

"Math, Andrei, and please, call me Nils. You're looking at an equation. It's like a heat map—the colors show intensities of the input values. It's the beauty that makes up our universe, Andrei.

"Math?" was his one-word response.

"These are visual representations of the Julia Set, a set of numbers that work in an equation. This one you will like even more, my friend," said Nils as he turned to a page near the middle of the book. Andrei traced his fingers over the spiraling shapes.

"It looks so familiar, like I've dreamed this page."

Aunt Vicky's voiced bounced into Nils' head. "Or lived it somewhere," he offered. "It's the Mandelbrot Set, another equation. Take a look at this one."

Andrei looked. His eyes drank in the color and winding shapes of the page. *Here. Right here,* he thought without speaking.

"That's Seahorse Valley, Andrei. I know how to get there. We don't have to dig, well not far."

Andrei looked up with the tired eyes of someone who hadn't been allowed to believe for such a long time.

"I always knew you were an explorer, Andrei. Come find this valley with me. Meet me in my office at the Assembly tomorrow evening, at 8. You will meet a business partner of mine from Paris. I can safely say that he, too, is interested in seahorses."

*

The next day, Marten the waiter/speechwriter/security detail approached with a tall chef's hat and a tray full of small glasses filled to the brim with clear liquid. "Aquavit or Wodka?" he demanded politely, his paper hat lightly scraping the ceiling of the pristine office. Andrei selected the drink of his host's homeland, only to find with the tiniest sip that it was merely a tiny glass of water.

Nils chuckled behind him in a group of high-backed chairs that faced the window. "We need clear minds tonight, Andrei. They're all water. And besides, Carl doesn't drink." At the mention of the other name, Andrei noticed an extra pair of feet below one of the chairs. No one stood up or made an introduction so Andrei walked over to the window, going around the chairs to meet their contents.

"Carl, meet Ambassador Andrei Soltanovsky of the Russian Federation. And Andrei, this is Dr. Carl Enders of the Goethe Institute in Paris." A hardy shaking of hands was bookended by silence and the overweight man did not get out of his chair.

Finally Andrei forced out, "I thought the Goethe Institute was in Germany."

"We're practically in Germany here, aren't we?" offered Nils letting his mind wander to the half-timbered houses in the city center. "Well, Carl feels decidedly more inspired in Paris and tends to take his work along with him." Andrei looked at Carl, who still had not said a word. He began to wonder how willing of a participant the doctor was in this meeting. "Come, sit, Andrei."

Nils flicked on a TV screen with a clunky beige remote and fed it a cassette. The apparatus, new when he first took office, now seemed like a dinosaur. An eerily beautiful picture appeared on screen, one reminiscent of paisley lace. The black and white shapes echoed the curves from the book, moving ever closer, the details remaining as intricate the whole way.

"These are zooms, Andrei. Close-ups of some of the equations from the book. You keep getting closer and closer and there's just more and more detail. You never get to the smallest unit. You see, Dr. Enders believes that we're all part of a 3-D version of one of these equations. Like the one containing seahorse valley."

Andrei chuckled, but couldn't take his eyes off the screen. "You live in this valley, Doctor? I find it quite beautiful, but I am confident that I am not a resident."

"Ambassador," came the voice of the chubby man on Nils' right side. "I am suggesting that there are far more equations to map. The Mandelbrot is one of perhaps an infinite number of sets. What we'd like to find out is which one we're in, which template we follow. Comprehending our place in the Cosmos is my life's goal, Ambassador. It's the only thing that drives me forward. Otherwise I'm always looking back."

"And what will you do, Doctor?" replied Andrei with a smirk. "What will you do when you know?"

"I suppose I'll call on an old friend," said Carl, his eyes cast downward.

"Well let's say I'm interested," questioned Andrei. "What do you need from me? I'm not sure my appreciation of your paisley seahorse art will be of much help."

"Nils has secured a site," said Carl, now looking excited by the prospect of the Ambassador's genuine interest, his full chin wobbling as he spoke. "It's part of one of his prison initiatives." Both men looked at Nils as he smiled and proudly held up his tiny glass of water in a toasting motion.

"So you're sending these magnificent seahorses to jail, Nils? I hardly think they deserve it," came Andrei's snarky reply. "I wonder—"

"It's for their protection, Andrei, and ours," interjected Nils between sips of water. "It really is lovely. Just outside of town, down the river in St. Kell. The site has full-time security and good cover. There's a deep basement too. There's less interference underground. It's perfect. But what we need are some brains and brawn to feed the project."

He turned his body to fully focus on Andrei and continued his explanation. "Carl has built a machine, a gorgeous machine. Well, the machine itself is not gorgeous, but what it does, oh, what it does is gorgeous."

"Gorgeous?"

"Gorgeous."

"So...what does it do?"

"Well, it reads, I guess. It picks up everything we can't see. It measures and records everything in our world, all in an effort to create a map. To figure out what we're part of. You see, Andrei, Carl and I are very curious. We want to know what the art in the air around us is made of. We want to know how our own world is built. We mean to reveal the math of its creation." Noting the confusion in the lines of Andrei's face, he added, "Carl, can you explain?"

"It's a translator, Mr. Ambassador. Or it will be. It takes data and translates it into something tangible that we can understand. I built it to play music from wavelengths of light, but Nils wants to make it stronger."

"Yes!" cried Nils, now on his feet and fully animated. "In fact, I want to make it much stronger. It will be able to process all the data and tell us what's going on here, measure even what we feel and experience, everything that happens. This machine will give us the equation of our universe. It's the ultimate level of understanding!" His eyes flashed with excitement as he continued his plea to Andrei.

"There's a lab in Lausanne with a true mad scientist, Andrei. He's brilliant like Carl and building a machine of his own. It's a computer with parallel processing just like the human brain. If we can get him to contribute a processor to our project, it will be like millions of minds working on this problem. It will surely speed up our work."

"I still don't understand my role, Nils. I don't know anything about computers, not much about brains either, to tell the truth."

"Yes, but *he* does. The Professor in Lausanne. I've already spoken with him, but he needs convincing from a non-European partner. He wants his tools to reach beyond the European Union and a Russian Ambassador might be just his ticket out. And of course there's the issue of cost. All that Swiss neutrality and cheese do not make up for EU cash. But the Assembly is grander because of its reach; both Switzerland and Russia can play in this club. You see, we've recently lost substantial funding from the Americans and even as an observer state, they were providing considerable resources. I've been informed that a voluntary contribution from the Russian Federation was submitted to the Assembly's general fund and has not yet been earmarked. Perhaps you could make prison reform one of the priorities of your diplomatic mission."

"And I thought it was only women who wanted me for me money," replied Andrei with a grin. "I'll see what I can do, Nils. I'll see what I can do. Now, on that note, can you please turn this water into wine?"

THE ARGENTINIAN
(2011)

Vicky Victoria had met her husband at her birth father's funeral. After five years of marriage, they would finally take a trip to India together. Viswanatha Suresh Venkataraman went back every year for Divali, but this time his wife would be by his side. They would wander the city streets, surrounded by old cows, eating pomegranates and mangoes. She would meet her mother in-law and wear the crisply starched, goldenrod sari that had been sent over, the one she'd never gotten around to trying on. Vicky's reservation had her returning to Minneapolis two weeks later. Suresh had a one-way ticket.

Suresh had become a citizen of the New World and thought he could leave the life of his youth behind. The heat, the smells, the people. So many people. But Mumbai was calling him back as surely as Vicky was pushing him away. They were perfect together, except that they weren't. His parents had probably been right, that he should have married another Manglik. He hadn't wanted Chandra Kundali to rule his life, but he could feel Mars smirking as he lurked in the 8th house of his horoscope chart.

Dr. Venkataraman's parents had found a Manglik bride for him before he slunk out like a coward on a red-eye to New York. He'd been applying for positions in the US for a year unbeknownst to his family, who loved him so much they wanted to script his life. Suresh never even met Dhanya, his perfect match, who woke up the morning of her wedding to find that her fiancé had left the country. Their disastrous energies associated with the Mangal Dosha were supposed to have cancelled each other out. Dhanya's family had been thrilled to find not only another Manglik, but a fellow doctor who spelled success and happy marriage for their daughter.

Since the food had already been ordered, Dhanya's family swallowed their pride and dramatically married her off to a tree, with all the guests to watch. She divorced the tree the same day, with her parents' blessing, and Suresh's brother sent a photo of the ceremony to Dr. Vicky, care of the St. Tabitha clinic in Minneapolis, Minnesota. This was the only photo Suresh had of his past life and it was displayed awkwardly by his front door: beautiful, round-faced young Indian dressed in red and gold, her sorrow masked by bright layers of makeup, standing next to a tree. Apparently the short arborious union cancelled Dhanya's bad energy and she was able to marry her secret boyfriend, who was neither doctor, nor Manglik, nor literate, but who made her smile with her eyes crinkled up.

Vicky knew the story, but didn't mind the woman who stared back at her just to the left of the door each morning, with her pile of gold chain necklaces glistening brightly in the sun. She liked to think that Suresh had left India for her, even though they hadn't met until Suresh had already been in the country for several months on his study visit. She continually batted away the idea that her husband had felt more for her late birth father than herself. Although she'd never remembered seeing Carl Enders in person, she looked into his grey eyes each day in the mirror and wondered if that was what Suresh loved about her. And now he was leaving her, just like he'd let that woman to marry a tree, without ever really knowing her.

When Suresh had decided to open a clinic with a childhood friend back in India, Vicky refused to leave her sister, Ping, and held her up as a shield from the truth: that she was no longer needed by her better half. The trip to Mumbai was to be a goodbye journey, one they had agreed would help them transition from one back to two. They would go for two weeks, visiting the haunts of Suresh's late night stories and gradually letting go. They had cried together after booking the tickets, until Vicky wiped the tears off Suresh's face and said, "I suppose you'll meet someone new there, my big, darling Manglik. I was just your tree." He laughed deep down, with a rumbling joy in his broad chest that hadn't fully escaped in five years.

"You are my twin star, Vicky, not my tree. It's in moving away from you and coming back that we will both gain understanding."

"Does that mean you'll be back?" she asked, doubtfully. She knew her question would launch Suresh into one of his Hindu-inspired musings on the way the world worked, but she was grateful for any of his sing-song chatter, which would soon be absent from her life.

"Time and its cycles are much longer than you'd expect, Vicky. Billions of years from now, Shiva will still be dancing. Brahma is dreaming of us, and you will dream many dreams within his. We'll meet again many times."

Vicky had been sleeping on the couch for three months, but the night they clicked to confirm the trip to India, she crawled in next to her grand husband as he slept. She wasn't sure if he was awake, but he put his heavy arm over her and she instantly fell asleep. By morning, his side of the bed was already cold. Vicky could smell tea brewing as she stood and walked to her husband, bathed in morning sun with a phone pressed to his ear. He looked up at Vicky as if he were looking right through her.

"Yes, I'll look at it right now. Did you send it to Vicky or to me? She's just awoken; I'll bring it to her attention immediately. Thank you, Mike. And thank you for your discretion." He put the phone down, but still didn't reach to her, instead opening his laptop and scrolling as he spoke to the screen.

"That was Mike Vickie. He received an email this morning, one that Victoria had advised him to discard. He's taken the liberty to forward it. You need to read this. It's about your father," Suresh said flatly as he turned the screen toward Vicky.

Vicky couldn't imagine any aspects of her life that were worthy of intervention by the US Senate so she gathered the forwarded email must have alluded to the delicate nature of her relationship with Victoria Vickie. They had been sisters for four years and then had their father ripped from their lives, not once, but twice. They'd come together for the funeral, but like two magnets turned the wrong way, they were constantly repelling.

Before reading the message, Vicky put her hand on her husband's forearm. "Suresh, Carl Enders is not my father. You've met my dad; he loves you. His name is Lothaire."

"I know, Vicky, but…" His face turned to the screen again. The couple continued to the message, forwarded despite matrimonial objection from Mike Vickie:

Dear Senator Vickie,

We briefly met at the funeral of my colleague and friend, Carl Enders: I'm not sure what your relation is to him, but at the very least as one of your constituents, I thought you should be concerned on both a

95

personal and professional level by the information I received from an acquaintance in Europe.

The Miscellaneous Society, of which I've just joined on the Board of Directors; appears to have been defrauded by someone claiming to be Carl. Our records indicate that he received a research grant in 1980 and traveled to Paris for follow-up work on color theory. His grant has been reviewed every four years since then and the address from his most recent application shows an address at a prison in eastern France. I dug around the local sources, but I'm not the best in French and have found virtually no trace of this impostor nor the reason for his imprisonment. However, my colleague at the Assembly of Europe's Ethics Committee was able to provide the translation of an announcement in his committee's newsletter archives:

> The European Court of Human Rights threw out the case of Carl Enders, an American physicist based in Paris, claiming that security concerns justified his living conditions in an underground cell at St. Kell Prison in a suburb of Strasbourg, France. Dr. Enders published on behalf of Upper Mississippi University and, most recently, the Miscellaneous Society. His work on color perception theory was the basis for the Goethe Institute's traveling exhibition, Frontiers of Chaos. Dr. Enders continues to be held at St. Kell for the remainder of his sentence.

I thought you should know that the Society has suspended funding pending an investigation, but the matter has not yet been pursued due to our own lack of personnel. The matter only came to my attention at a board meeting this week and I found the situation presented a rather alarming upset to our normally mundane meeting minutes.

On a personal note, Mr. Enders' wife, Claire Méndez, contacted me several years ago to inquire about his whereabouts. That was before his death, but I never managed to locate her when the Star Tribune published the notice of his burial. I hope to bring peace to Carl's upended family and hope your office can provide some insight into this matter.

Kind regards,
Marka Swandish

Vicky looked up to Suresh. "This is not the Carl Enders you knew. It's certainly not anyone I know. Who cares?"

"I watched him die, Vicky; I saw the life drain out all at once. Your birth father is dead, I'm sure of it. I just wonder why someone would find it appealing to walk in his shoes. It certainly hasn't gained him any favor."

Vicky smiled. She loved the way Suresh, her broad and brilliant husband, wove words around, making all his statements sound both musical and slightly awkward.

"Well, I for one, don't want to know," said Vicky with minimal conviction. Except that she did.

*

Vicky and Suresh were checked into a cramped hotel on a pedestrian street that angled down from the Strasbourg cathedral. They'd arrived in the afternoon with little experience in jet lag and were feeling the walls start to curve with fatigue. Suresh muttered about the impact of light exposure on melatonin as Vicky's eyes gave up resistance and began to blur.

Suresh put a heavy, but tender, hand on Vicky's back, shepherding her from side to side. "We just need to stay up another three hours and tomorrow we'll be fine." He dragged her into her second wind by securing a small glass in her floppy hand. Vicky looked down at the *kir*, white wine tinged lavender by currant syrup, in a glass ringed by tiny painted-on children holding hands. Somehow they'd made it across the street to a restaurant.

They were in a warm dining hall over-decorated with Alsatian folklore — the same laboriously cheery children half-grinned back at them from several corners of the great room. Storks, tall almond cakes, round red hearts and cartoonish pretzels left little room for conversation, not that Vicky had much left to say.

A waiter came after several hollow and humid minutes, insisting that the bacon in the vegetarian plate was just for flavor and could by no means be removed. And so Vicky and Suresh embarked on another journey within their own—a tour of France in cheeses. The waiter brought himself to the brink of tears talking about the summer grass that only 4 authorized cows could graze on a particular patch of heaven in Limousin, resulting in the fluffy white disk before them. Vicky's eyes were losing the power to focus again as she ascertained that the server loved these distant cows even more than her husband had loved either her or her dead father.

The jealousy that Vicky suddenly felt toward a nameless bovine drove her to call back the circle of children that encased liquid respite. By glass four she was unexpectedly awake and eager to grab familiar hands across the table. "Don't go to Mumbai, Suresh. I'm not ready to lose you yet."

"You lost me before you found me, Vicky. In there," he said, dragging her hands in his so he could point to the ring of children on the wineglass. "And there." He didn't point this time, but only looked to Vicky's face. They both knew he was referring to her side relationship with pharmaceuticals, the lover who never left. Vicky knew Suresh could pity her, but could never understand. It didn't seem fair that he could be so good. That he could revel in baklava, honey dripping from his smile, without that voice that whispered *one more*. Suresh never required a second hit.

Changing the topic to her sister, Suresh asked, "Do you want to call Ping? See if she made it there?" A friend at a travel agency had agreed last minute to change the Mumbai reservation from Vicky Victoria to Ping Victoria, so that the ticket wouldn't be wasted. Ping had always wanted to travel and Suresh's parents were more than happy to host their son's soon to be estranged sister in-law, if for no better reason than to highlight their unwavering commitment to family, feeling that it would offset Suresh's habit of leaving women behind. Ping would weave baskets with Suresh's cousin for two weeks.

"No, I'll see her when she gets back. I'll probably just start blubbering if I talk to her." Suresh had never quite appreciated Vicky's inconvenient attachment to Ping since normally a day didn't go by without a quick visit or a lengthy phone call to pull her out of whatever funk she had sunken into.

"I never told you this before, Vicky, but, you know how you think you saved her? With the yin and yang and everything? I did believe you. I'm sorry I laughed about it when you told me back then. I do think it's possible. So much is possible that we don't understand yet. I know that you carry the pain of two souls, day and night, and it has made you so tired. I love my sister too and I would take all the dark from her if I had to. But I don't think it was Ping that you helped. She's fine, Vicky; she's always been fine." Half glaring and half adoring, Vicky gazed back over the table and didn't speak. "I believe you saved Victoria. She is still your sister after all. You're the reason she survived. You're the reason she kept smiling as family after family passed her by at the orphanage. That's why she's the superman, sweet one."

They progressed to a pitcher of Sylvaner as Suresh's final term of endearment dispersed in the ether. "You're like Asha and Lata, you two," he added, but Vicky missed, as often, the obscure Indian reference. The waiter equipped Suresh with a glass to help the effort before tomorrow's visit to St. Kell Prison.

*

A determined pink glow the color of the previous night's aperitif seeped up from the horizon. "Is that sunrise or sunset, Suresh?" Vicky's head pounded as she realized she had no comprehension of the time or space she was in.

Suresh groaned, "Well, is it getting lighter or darker?"

"I can't tell," said Vicky as she got up and walked barefoot down an uneven hallway and out the door of the hotel. There was neither the bustle of morning nor the chatter of evening. Just pink light and emptiness on the cobblestone street. But a low clunking tone that she swore was a cowbell could be heard and she half expected an animal to appear, one of the glowing night friends that had visited her as a child, a cow walking around the cobblestones that should have been Mumbai. She turned back to the hotel and ran down the hall to curl up next to Suresh, pondering his well-built leg that stuck out of the sheets. It had been wrapped around her a few hours ago, but she couldn't remember how he'd pushed into her a final time, shoveling dirt over their matrimony.

Vicky looked to the hotel dresser and saw a collection of the folk-child wineglasses, two nearly full, on top. Apparently Suresh was more kleptophilic in his rare moments of inebriation and had stuffed several empty glasses into Vicky's purse too. Now with clear eyes and thumping head she could read the melancholy on the Alsatian children's faces that she'd overlooked the night before, the survival-mode gaze of creatures born into a violent and seemingly-endless tug-of-war between France and Germany. These weren't kids who screamed with glee in hide-a-beds and begged for more rainbow sherbet. These were children she could relate to. She moved her gaze up to the window and the miniscule balcony beyond. What she'd heard as a cowbell was a rusty set of windchimes, hanging from an iron stork that looked like it was flying in the morning air.

*

Vicky held Suresh's hand loosely in the tram from downtown to St. Kell, a neighborhood to the south of Strasbourg. As they left the city center, the buildings gradually showed more sign of wear. Chocolate boutiques gave way to hair extension salons, then televised horse-racing bars with shredded awnings. Just before arriving, there was a stretch of boarded up homes along the tram line in what looked like no-man's land. Finally, they passed under a bridge and rounded a corner until the tram came to a stop. A scratchy voice came out of an unseen speaker. "Kellersdorff-Saint-Charles-sur-Argent-le-Neuf. *Terminus.*"

Suresh reclaimed his sweaty hand and stepped out with Vicky. The tram pulled away to reveal a boarded-up supermarket and little else. A sign indicating the Saint Kell Prison led them a mere block over to the barbed-wire wall. A uniformed man in a booth sat expressionless as Vicky tried to explain the reason of their visit. She repeated, "Carl Enders" and "I'm his daughter," three times before the man slid a small paper form under a plexiglass barrier.

"Oh, Vicky, remember you have this," came the reassuring tone of Suresh's voice from behind. He pulled open his travel file and amazed Vicky with his organizational skills for the umpteenth time. "Here," he said as he handed her the letter that Senator Vickie's office had painstakingly prepared in English and French on her behalf, unbeknownst to the Senator's wife. Vicky slid it to the mum guard, who looked it over briefly and shook his head.

"*Non,*" he said authoritatively, but without expounding. He clearly was not in the mood to speak, much less explain in English, and he must have assumed that by fixing his stare at a spot on the counter in front of him that the couple they would eventually leave.

"Um, *s'il vous plait, visite?* Monsieur Enders?" she tried once more. The man looked up at her and sighed, then tapped his meaty finger where 'Carl Enders' was written on the page.

"No visit. No visit for Enders. No."

"*Pourquoi pas?*" demanded Vicky, although she was certain her one semester of French would not provide understanding in the event that the guard became more loquacious. The sausage finger moved from Carl's name to a square button on the side of the desk. Almost immediately, two officers appeared in tight, cable knit police sweaters. They each took an elbow of the pair and firmly marched them away from the booth. The man inside yelled something at the officers and they turned around. The one holding Vicky's elbow let go and bounded back to the booth as the man inside shoved a paper back through. The officer delivered the senator's letter back to Vicky's hand and performed a very slight bow with his head.

"*Au revoir,*" the two officers said together when they had sufficiently distanced the pair from the prison, then turned around and disappeared behind a concrete wall.

Vicky and Suresh looked around, not sure what to do, when they noticed a man holding a cardboard box on the doorstep of an old house that looked like an appendage of the prison. A tiny plume of smoke wafted from the man. They couldn't tell how long he'd been there, but he smiled when they looked his way. He'd been waiting to be noticed, with a hand-rolled cigarette dangling out of his mouth and dropping bits of ash onto the box. He put the box down and walked a few steps over to the couple, transferring the cigarette to his left hand. Suresh asked the man if he lived there.

"No, this my grandmother house. She die last year and we need to empty it. They will knock it down, build apartments. Very nice. Prison-view apartments. Almost as good as being on other side," he said with a smirk. His English was lightly accented, but didn't sound very French.

"I am Nicolas Arbogast," he continued. "So, you look for Dr. Enders? He is not a prisoner. He's here all day, sometimes all night, but he gets paid to be here, see the difference?"

"He works here?" Vicky and Suresh said in unison. The couple who had never completed one another's sentences had accomplished their first jinx.

"If you help me to carry some boxes, I show you how to find him."

Suresh and Vicky looked at each other in tacit agreement. After all, they didn't have many options at this point. Suresh stuck out his hand for the strange gentleman in the powder blue track suit. "I'm Viswanatha Venkataraman and this is my wife, Vicky." Nicolas Arbogast eyed the woman in front of him, sizing her up in the most obvious way as he shook Suresh's hand, but she didn't notice as she was still reeling from being called a wife this late in the game.

"Vicky, you say? And this Doctor is your father." He looked like he was trying to keep a eureka moment under wraps, his dark eyes just slightly widening then shrinking again. "I have maybe someone else to introduce you to. I think you will like her; she live underground. Want to meet her?"

Vicky looked at the man as he unrolled the one pushed-up cuff of his pastel pant leg. She picked up a cardboard box from the stoop as her answer, surprised by its weight. A ceramic Jesus figurine peeked through the gap in the cardboard, his face painted slightly off-center.

Nicolas disappeared into the old house and returned to the door with two larger boxes that blocked his face from view. Suresh hurried to grab one as the man started to teeter. It was obviously the dimensions of the boxes that were problematic and not their heft. Vicky could make out an astounding array of muscles under the baby-blue top. She walked directly behind Nicolas so she could watch the changing shape of them with each movement.

They carried the boxes just a few meters before turning down the street. The wide pavement was empty and a bus shelter on the left was surrounded by shards of broken glass. After two minutes they reached a river. There was a children's playground, tagged with spray paint that lacked any artistic flair and looked more like black territorial piss.

But the river reclaimed everything that was wrong with the strange prison quarter. The million flecks of light bouncing off the surface looked like living silver. It was so bright, but Vicky didn't want to look away, so she continued in a straight line with her heavy box, her eyes closed, but aimed at the river. The flashes from the surface of the water were only slightly dimmed by her eyelids. Suresh looked around at the houses that had somehow escaped most of the desolation found just one street over. Immaculate gardens were still in full bloom well into autumn.

After five minutes, they arrived at a big, white house with a round tower on the left side. "*Bienvenue chez moi*," said Nicolas as Suresh took in the height of the tower. Its stature did not seem to correlate to the young man's economic status. "Yeah, it's big," said Nicolas to the question no one had asked. "But it belongs to no one, or no one I know. No one tell me to move out." Suresh gathered that the squatter must have lived in his grandmother's house until some point before installing himself in the abandoned 70s mansion down the street.

The house was unsettlingly empty. The huge, round room that was visible from the outside as the tower had wooden slats covering the windows so that only fine lines of daylight came through. A mattress lay in the center of the room, its blankets drawn flat and folded back at the top. Nicolas had no furniture, but he made his bed. Built-in wooden bookshelves were full with books going the wrong direction, stacked in heaps with horizontal spines. The trio put their boxes down and Nicolas offered up some warm orange soda, which was refused by both and accepted enthusiastically by Nicolas himself. With orange lips, he led them towards a stairway flanked by two metal statues of young boys.

"Who's the welcome committee?" asked Vicky.

"This Nico and Mo. See?" he said as he posed next to one with a scraped metal cheek. Vicky noticed the scrape just as she noticed a long, light scar in the same place on Nicolas' face. "It's me. And this is my…how do call it? A step brother? He's the guy who marry my sister."

"Your brother in-law."

"Yeah, so say hi to my brother in-law and we continue." Vicky looked at the other metal boy, taking in the metal stump that was his sawed-off appendage.

"Hi Mo, what happened to your hand?" said Suresh, but neither Nicolas nor the metal Mo answered so he continued down the stairs.

He brought them through a type of dark that inspired clinging-on and, although her kindhearted defector was close behind, it was Nico that Vicky was drawn to. She held back and kept her hands running along the wall, feeling her way along and willing herself to accept being alone. At least for this instant, at least for this life. Making it through this tunnel would prove she'd make it through others. It felt like she'd taken this journey in the dark a thousand times, each turn equally familiar. Left, left, now right and left again. Going above ground and back under openly disoriented Suresh, but Vicky was a giant finger retracing age-old paths on a map in her mind. Left, left. Right. Left.

A blue light this far underground startled Suresh and he held back as Vicky walked up to a great machine, placing her hands on it to feel its warmth.

"What is it?" she asked over her shoulder to Nicolas.

"You really don't know? Your father make her."

Vicky first though he was getting his pronouns wrong until he continued, "looks like he name her after you." Nicolas pointed to something and Vicky brought her face closer to read a small green tag: Vicki 4.0

Her heart thumped past the beat it was meant to hit and sped up. She suddenly felt trapped, deep underground with a stranger who was looking for explanations she couldn't provide. Thankfully, Suresh stepped closer and spoke. "We'd like to talk to Dr. Enders now, please. In fact, he's the only reason we came." Vicky rummaged through his statement, dissecting the meaning. *The only reason.*

"Okay, okay," said Nicolas, "but I visit Vicki at night, see? The doctor doesn't know I'm here. I show you where he works and he comes a bit later. You don't tell him I bring you here. Good?"

"Good," the husband and wife replied together; they were getting better at this.

*

Nicolas had deposited them, via a small elevator, directly into Carl Enders' office, which was contained inside the walls of St. Kell Prison. They were to leave the prison the conventional way and come back to Nicolas' place once they were done. He instructed them to bar any mention of how they had arrived via tunnel, stressing that breaking into jail could get them in more trouble than breaking out.

Carl Enders was nearly startled out of his suit as he walked into his office an hour later to the sight of two strangers. It looked like the three-piece corduroy number had been squeezed too hard, squirting a frantic, jowled head up through its starched collar. He jumped to the desk phone, but before he could dial, Suresh laid a massive hand on his shoulder and said, "Carl, this is one of the daughters you left behind in America. Her name is Vicky."

A look of panic came over the man's dark and pudgy, lined face as he looked back and forth from Vicky to Suresh. He stood frozen with the phone still in his hand. Suresh took his own hand off the doctor and continued, "It's alright, Carl, we're just looking for an explanation. You don't appear to be who you think you are."

Carl Enders sank down to a sitting position on the edge of his desk, putting the phone back down. His eyes darted quickly back and forth as the floodgate opened and a tale unfolded from its own type of prison:

"Okay, okay. Carlos Michel Chazal. My grandparents were from Paris, my whole family actually, but I was born in Argentina. I was born Carlos."

Vicky looked from Suresh and back to the imposter again, who was already continuing while simultaneously examining his ripped cuticles.

"Where my parents tried to assimilate, my grandfather and grandmother lived with a foot in the life they left behind. When I was growing up, I thought I was French. That's what Mami and Papi always told me. All their bedtime stories were about the city of lights. All their lullabies, all their food. I'm not even sure why they left if they loved it so much. It was the tale of a film house in Paris that made me come here. I felt like I was just coming back to somewhere I always was."

Vicky was still hovering awkwardly in the middle of the office with Suresh, the only furniture being the desk, which was partially covered in the Argentinian's left buttock. She longed to tell Carl that she didn't care why he came here, that she just wanted enough of an explanation to satisfy Suresh's curiosity and close the case. But Carl's shabby hands started to pick at themselves and the speech continued.

"I was different from other kids, not just because of my clothes or the Sunday dinners we had. I was profoundly different and I didn't know why, but Papi and Mami said I had un *atout*. They acted like everything weird about me was a good thing, a gift. I could hear colors, already back then even, and sometimes, sometimes they were screaming. Papi told me someone just needed to understand the colors, to teach them how to sing. He told me about the most fantastic colors he had ever seen, in a Paris film house before they'd left for Argentina. There was a film called *Voyage dans la Lune* and the colors were something he couldn't even describe for their beauty. I kept that tucked in the back of my mind for decades, always wondering what those colors in the film would sound like, whether they would blend together or churn around each other like all the rest."

Carl's monologue seemed far from closing, so Vicky pulled herself down to a comfortable squat, hovering inches above a Persian carpet in the otherwise bereft office. She tugged Suresh down with her and he crossed his legs like a schoolboy at her side as Carl's story continued.

"Well I didn't make it to Paris straight away. I got there slowly, not that I'm complaining about the journey. I went to Minnesota, where you were born, Vicky, to work in a lab with Dr. Marka Swandish. She sponsored me for an internship and she was everything I could ever hope to be. She was inquisitive and rational at the same time. I wanted to work like her, to be like her, as she unraveled the fabric of the universe. Marka was a sorcerer to me, but not an evil one. She was so strong and determined that she made us all forget what a joke we were working on. Marka held us up; she stayed up two nights in a row writing a grant application for me to build my first machine. But I didn't build it for her. I built it for your father, Carl Enders.

"We were both fairly anonymous in Marka's shadow back then. We were both named Carlos so most people thought of us as the same anyway. To the outside world, it wasn't a leap to become him. But, my god, how we were different. Carl Enders was born Carlos, just like me. I thought of it as just changing a name to fit the geography. If I had been born in France, I'd be Charles, in Argentina I was Carlos and in America I became Carl. But for Carl Enders, changing his name from Carlos Méndez was a step away from something he was, a way to forget where he came from, a way to hide in plain sight.

"I knew in 1958, on a vacation in Montevideo, what Carl pushed back for a lifetime. Now that was a beautiful film house. Montevideo! I went to see the topless Isabel Sarli in *El trueno entre las hojas*. It was meant to be scandalous, sneaking into the theater to ogle her in the swimming hole, but all I found myself staring at were the shirtless Indians. I didn't waste my time with Catholic guilt like he did. I knew what I knew and embraced it. Carl was so young, married to your mother and living with a particular kind of woe that couldn't be shared. But he loved me. He loved me in the way you can't speak about because it just cheapens it, makes it play movies in your mind. But Carl loved the whole of me, even all the voices that wailed at me from the dark. But to really know me, I wanted to make him hear them too. I had to."

Vicky could see drops of blood forming on Carl's hands as he tugged his cuticles and refused to look up. His voice continued steadily and he started to rub the blood around his fingertips, as if even distribution meant removal.

"What I built is based on the Victrola my Papi brought from Paris. He and Mami had sacrificed nearly their entire wardrobe for a chance to load that machine on the steamer and bring it to Argentina. I imagined myself like the little stylus, riding the waves of the music that the patterns made on the record, amplifying them, translating them to human ears. Carl's the one who named the Vicki, before I even started building it. Before Nils inspired me to re-build her on the Old Continent as Vicki 2.0. You and your sister were the only thing Carl talked about besides work; he thought you were

106

magical. You were always pulling him back, pulling him away from me. Looking back, I think he named it after you more than my phonograph. He was thinking of you all the time. Every waking moment. Except—" Carl made a theatrical pause and turned his hand over as though offering something to Vicky, finally looking down to where she hovered over the rug.

"Except that I'm not her. How did you know?"

Carl smiled in contempt with puffy lips. "Vicky is the Superman. She can see more colors than most people. You're clearly that grumpy imp Laney, all grown up, but still a lump of darkness. You're just like a little black hole. No light could escape—" Carl was cut off by Suresh in a rare angry voice reserved for broken dish quarrels in the wee hours. He had somehow pulled himself to standing in a split second.

"What do you mean, she can see more colors?" he asked, now peering down at Carl, who had moved on to picking at the other hand.

"She sees more because Carl Enders sees less. Always a martyr, that dear man. See, Carl Enders, the real one, is colorblind. Not completely, but he has what's called a deuteranomaly. He can't see green. And not only does he want to see green, he wants to see all the impossible colors, the supergreens and the bluish yellows. It's not even fair to be handicapped by one's own eyes. Part of his world is missing. But he knows there is more to see, even more than Vicky can see. As his daughter, she's a carrier for deuteranomaly, but it gave her an extra cone in her eye, which makes her a tetrachromat. She has four cones instead of three and she can pick up millions of colors that the rest of us can't see. But I can hear them, I know they're there. That's what I'm working on, that's what carries me forward. I'm going to show Carl what the universe is made of, show him all the colors."

An awkward silence passed through as Vicky and Suresh realized the weight of this man's present tense speech. He was obviously unaware of Carl's high-speed collision with a rock and his current location below the Mexican soil.

"And where do you think you'll find him, Carl?" came Suresh's voice, lower and saturated with compassion this time. He had only felt the early pangs of adoration for Dr. Enders, but the man before him had become fully absorbed.

"If you must know, I find him every time I light a candle for him, in Notre

Dame. We used to light a candle for Carl's mother back in the Cathedral of Saint Paul once in a while. Now I light them for Carl, in Paris. I imagine he'd like the symbolism. So I wait in line with all those Chinese tourists toting Vuitton bags so I can keep the light glowing for him. Well, I did, anyway, until I got to Strasbourg." Something told Vicky the doctor was every bit a prisoner here as the inmates, but she didn't know if he was being held by Nils or had imposed the confinement on himself. "Maybe you could do that for me if you ever make it Paris. Now that I'm down here, I mean. Maybe you could light a candle for your father." Vicky felt that she owed nothing to this underground stranger, but merely nodded her head at his suggestion as he continued.

"The real Carl Enders, if you're looking for him, is in Minneapolis. They're taking care of him well, the best they can anyway. They have awfully boring films there, but he's safe. I went to see him before I left. He didn't know I was there. I pretended to be visiting his roommate, an immobile fellow who liked soup. I just kept spooning it in, spooning it in as I peeked at Carl across the table. That hole in his head was no third eye, if you catch my drift. I don't think it worked out quite how he'd planned. Anyway, I think I could have gone right up to him and sat in his lap and he wouldn't have noticed. But he'll wake up when he hears what's humming around him. When he finally understands."

Suresh finally stepped in. "How could you leave him there? At Saint Tabitha's? That place nearly killed him. If you loved him so much, how could you run off to Paris without him? Calling yourself a doctor is a disgrace to the profession."

"So you do know St. Tab?" replied Carl. He paused to consider either the question or the answer. "I left him there to be him. To live for him. I'm bringing his work forward. Our work. And it's not that I loved him. I love him now, still. I'm coming back for him. You look at me like I'm an old, fat man. Pathetic. But there are still projects up here." He tapped the side of his head for effect. "I'll return his passport, his identity, anything he wants. I'll be anyone he wants, but not for a vegetable. I need the music to wake him up. And the Vicki, the first one, it's not strong enough. It would never do for this task, so we're making it more capable, more like your Superman. We're almost ready."

Suresh looked at the engineer gone awry and put his hand out to pull Vicky up from the floor. "I think we have heard enough, Carl. But, tell me one last thing, did you ever see that film in Paris? Did you take your trip to the moon?"

Carl's eyes narrowed, creasing his whole flabby face. "I went to see it, yes. They play it at the same film house from time to time, even still today. But there were no colors; I don't know what my grandparents meant by that. It was a silent film in every way imaginable. A silent film in black and white."

*

Something about the second Carl Enders making his way into Vicky's life disturbed her. He reminded her of someone, but she couldn't place who it was. Or maybe it was the way he cared so deeply for her birth father, loved him in a way she'd never experience.

"Did you love Carl too, Suresh? Like the Argentinian loved him? Why else would you come all this way?"

"I loved something about him, Vicky, but no, I'm not completely won over by the affections of men. It's just…Carl Enders woke me up somehow, not the other way around. He reminded me of someone dear to me as a child, a kind of spiritual guide. He made me question every moment, doubt every truth."

"I guess he taught you to question me. He's not my father, Suresh."

"Yes, Vicky. Laney. He was. He is your father. He tried so hard to get you back. He didn't choose his path."

"You mean a power drill with a one-inch bore disk isn't choosing a path? Forgive me if I fail to understand. All any of you are good for is leaving. That's all you know how to do. When the ride was rough, he let go and you admire him for that. And now you're letting go of me."

Suresh's tight hug was his answer. But every embrace has a release and before Vicky could register the loud click of the hotel clock, he was packing his bag for a life without her.

"Has it been 4 days already?"

Suresh stopped neatly folding his clothes to look at Vicky. "Yesterday was not a good day, my lamb. You let it pass too fast." This was his gentle way of saying she'd stumbled through the most important day of Divali in a chemical cloud. Suresh picked up a book from beside a tiny statue of Ganesha on the table. His fingers were yellow with spices and the smell of

109

long-burning candles hung in the air from an annual ceremony Vicky had never cared to understand, performed the night before. "You are caught up in the Maya, my love, hiding in the dark. I let some light in for you last night, my dear wanderer," he said as he came closer with the book.

"The day after Lakshmi Puja a husband gives his wife a gift. I'm sorry I put if off so many times." He handed her the book, a thin, worn *Rime of the Ancient Mariner*. "Your father spoke of this in his sleep. I think his curiosity, his comprehension of the universe was the albatross that hung from his neck."

"Thank you for the book, but you don't have to add any more meaning to this, Suresh. Just get going if you're going. Call me when you get to Mumbai."

"Shall I call you shouting from the Chhatrapati Shivaji Terminus?" Vicky sensed this was a well-worn joke between them from a hazier moment, but she couldn't quite piece it together.

"Call me when you're with Ping. I miss her."

Suresh's terms of endearment increased as he got closer to the door. "Okay, *mon chou*. That's what I would have called you if we had both been born here, in France. It means cabbage," he said with a smile.

"It sounds like a shoe, Suresh. You can just call me my name."

"Oh, but Vicky, you have so many names. Be sure to read the part I marked, *chérie*." He bent slightly to kiss her forehead, but low, almost between the eyes. His lips were red in the center as he parted them in a final genuine smile and turned away, floating out door.

Vicky looked into the tiny bathroom mirror and saw that Suresh had marked her with a Bindi, now slightly smeared by his mouth. She sat down on the bed and read the passage over and over, until the words looked foreign and danced across the page:

> Around, around flew each sweet sound,
> Then drifted to the sun,
> Slowly the sounds came back again
> Now mixed, now one by one.

*

Suresh had been gone for only a month, but Vicky had already forgotten his face somehow. Ping had called with a story about giving her prosthetic leg to a beggar down the road from Suresh's parents. She was staying in India, she'd said, at least for a while. With no Ping to go home to, no great Manglik arms to hold her steady, Vicky extended her stay in St. Kell. More precisely, she stayed in a neatly made bed in the middle of a round room next to ropy-muscled man that persistently smelled like gasoline. Vicky liked to think that her reinvention as a French squatter brought her closer to Ping, who by now was off the radar and happily sleeping on the hood of a car in Mumbai, her one leg blissfully dangling over the fender.

Nico, with no discernible employment, somehow kept cheese in the fridge and hash in a hollow book on the shelf. Without a bit of smoke, his speech became curt and cryptic. "I sell things," was his answer for the steady supply of dairy.

"My sister," was his brief explanation for his knowledge of English.

"I'm Arbogast," for why he didn't get kicked out of the abandoned house or get comments about the extension cord running from a neighbor's house in through the dog door to power Nico's cell phone.

"No," with a laugh when asked if he spoke Turkish.

Replies continued, succinct and lacking, unless the book/storage unit had been recently opened, like it had at dusk as they were sitting once again at sunset on a bench by the river. The bench was intended for banned products, like the red wine that never seemed to run out of supply in the cellar of the house, interspersed on dusty shelves with animal craniums from the previous homeowner. Her drinks were haram and could be imbibed on the bench, but not in the big white house. Finding no applicable words of wisdom from Muhammad on the subject of pills, Fentanyl and Demerol were always welcome dinner guests. And although Nico had confirmed that what he called *du shit* would technically be permitted inside, he didn't want the walls to go beige and sticky from the resin so he took his *shit*, which sounded more like "sheet," outside. In these instances, a little glob of hash was rolled on his thigh into a tiny worm, then sprinkled with loose tobacco for his unfiltered pleasure. Nico's stained fingers briefly reminded her of Suresh, but their hue was browner than turmeric or saffron.

Anticipating the explosion of vocabulary that would accompany the joint,

Vicky decided sunsets were the time to make more complex inquiries, and asked why he identified more with Islam than the Catholicism he'd been born into. The words floated out with the smoke that passed from his mouth to Vicky's.

"My God supposed to walk on water. And look." He gestured with an open hand at the glowing orange-pink orb of the sun and the rippling path it left on the surface of the water as it set, long and straight. "There he is, taking walk across the Argent. My sister, Marianne, she say our god – the church, the pottery Jesus in Mamama's room—all of it just to worship the sun. God of the Jews is a big ball of gas."

"So, you think your God is more real, Nico?" she asked. The hash from the good book tended to make her more alert than her pills did. They were becoming fast friends.

"Allah? I think they all the same guy, all the way back to Mithras, Buddah, all the old greats. They hum the same tune. Muhammad has some lyrics, just newer. I think that mean he have more backsight? Hindsight? And he's clear when he tell me what to do."

"What do you mean, Nico? What are you supposed to do?"

The joint burnt out along with Nico's ability to utter more than three consecutive words. "Save the world," he replied before the two returned to the great white house for an extended trial of sexual positions neither had yet endeavored.

Vicky woke in the middle of the night to find the bed empty. A familiar feeling of abandonment pulsed through her until she heard Nico tiptoeing through the round room and crawling next to her as she pretended to sleep. He put an arm around her, his hand smelling even stronger of solvent than usual.

"What are you doing walking around in the dark, Nico?" she said, sitting up.

"Working," said Nico as he pulled her warm body down to his cold one. "Go to sleep."

The connection to the burnt-out neighbor's car parked in the street was not immediately made. Doubts about the strange man by the river were pushed away by Vicky's fascination with Nico. She welcomed his rough hands and compact frame, if for nothing more than the contrast to the gentle giant who had discarded her. He cooked meals with a tiny hotplate, unplugging his sole source of electricity that powered his lamp and telephone to cook before it was too dark. They ate pretty much any produce they could salvage from the rejects of the Turkish market on the north side of the square, a business run entirely from the rejected products of the Turkish market on the south side of the square. But even moldy fruit and rock-hard bread tasted good next to Nico.

He would leave for hours at a time, sometimes overnight. They hadn't been underground since that first time he'd delivered her to the Argentinian, but she was sure that was where he went at least some of the time. They didn't speak much, but sometimes they would stare at each other in the low light just long enough to make perceptible changes to each other's irises. They reflected each other like enhanced mirrors and Vicky could almost feel his scar cut into her own cheek.

THE ABYSS
(2011)

It was the emptiness of the house in Nico's absence that made Vicky think about the Argentinian, how he wanted to be a needle on a record player. How she wished she could be content just letting the world spin around her, creating melodies just because she was there. And for the first time since arriving in St. Kell, she thought about her life back home—her emails, phone calls, full-color advertisements that filled her mailbox—so much information flowing into the abyss. She had spent so much of her life already letting her world spin and she wanted to be the one to make it turn now.

Nico was still gone when she heard the bell start to ring, a cast-iron clang that was unfamiliar in the white house. Vicky walked to the heavy front door and as she got closer heard knocking. She opened the door to find a handsome old man with ice-blue eyes and white hair, his leather-gloved hand holding the chain that powered the bell. He'd been both knocking and ringing simultaneously.

"Laney Enders, I've heard so much about you. The doctor tells me you've been to see him. You know, I always appreciate guests who use the front door," said the well-dressed man as he charged past Vicky into the house. He stopped abruptly, removed a glove and held out his hand. "Nils Winter's the name. May I come in? Oh, look at that, I'm already in. May I stay a moment? I wouldn't mind a tea. Or coffee, whatever you have that's hot."

Vicky went to the kitchen and returned with a glass of tap water. While electricity was procured from a neighbor, no one had thought to shut off the water supply. "I don't have anything hot," she said, putting the glass in Nils' hand. He made his way to the bare living room, where he set down his glass on the floor and began tugging on various chains to pull up the wooden blinds. Vicky was surprised to see the room bathed in natural light. Her eyes had grown accustomed to the dimness of her temporary world and she had imagined the floor much darker. Nils Winter noticed her looking down at his glass and walked over, placing a finger under her chin. He pulled upward until Vicky's eyes met his.

"The doctor tells me you've paid him a visit. Carl has explained his situation and I find very little issue in him re-purposing your father's name, given the circumstances. It was essential that he continue his work, not dwell on your father and his holey head. And he needed Carl Enders' passport to come here for the work; I can't imagine an Argentine passport would do for relocation during his, um, moment of need." He could see the fire catching in Vicky's eyes and he released her chin. "Oh, you're upset that he abandoned Carl Enders, maybe abandoned you in some way. But it was your mother who left, not Carl."

"I'm not sure who you're referring to; my mother was always very kind and teaches photography. And the woman who gave birth to me is dead. I don't remember a thing about her."

"I'm under the impression that she could stir up some memories whenever she liked. Even find you if she wanted to. I found you from all the way over here. Marka Swandish didn't get her information on Carl by chance. I tried to reach out to your sister, you know, via the Senator. I thought we could use those eyes of hers for the project. But she sent you. Why is that, Laney?"

"She didn't send me. She doesn't even know I'm here, not that she'd care either way. We're not...close. It was her husband who contacted me. And it's Vicky. Vicky Victoria."

"Yes, you are quite familiar with the practice of stealing identities yourself. It seems at some level you always wanted to be your sister, am I right? I'm not sure you should be so critical of the doctor. He met you once, when you were a child, did he mention that? You came to the lab once with your father while he was still working there."

"He said something like that, but I don't remember meeting him. I don't even remember the real Carl Enders, much less the fake one."

"He was working with your father on falsely coloring some images their boss had taken from the beyond, from outer space. The Pillars of the Universe. They were enhanced by a computer to show different types of gases where stars were forming and Carlos was showing them to you girls, plying you with candy in Marka's office so Carl could finish his code. Your father came running when he heard screaming; he thought maybe Marka was hurting your sister somehow. His greatest fear was someone using his daughter for her abilities…or misusing her. She was lying on the floor, crying from what she saw. She said it scared her."

Crying. Vicky could see it now. That bright, shining Victoria Vickie, her eternally blissful twin by birth had cried once in her life and she remembered. She remembered the tall woman with a great puff of hair hugging her sister tight on the floor of her office as she sobbed about the colors.

"The woman, Marka? She wasn't hurting her. Vicky was just so afraid, afraid of what she was seeing. She didn't know what it meant."

"But you didn't cry, did you, Laney? You were just fine because you couldn't see what she saw. Little Vicky was so special that way."

Vicky drew in a shaky breath. "But I did see it. Only, I wasn't scared. It was the most beautiful thing I've ever seen, more beautiful than anything I could imagine." She closed her eyes and continued. "The colors were folding inward, collapsing on each other, but always coming out whole, in thin, tangled ribbons at lightning speed. I can see them like they were painted on the backs of my eyelids. I remember."

"And that," said Nils with a smile like an outstretched hand, "that is why you're here, my dear."

*

Sometime later and several meters lower, Nils Winter had positioned himself between Vicky and the Vicki. "This machine has been considerably augmented by a special processor. It's modeled after a human brain. It uses parallel, rather than serial, processing. The Russians have contributed their discretionary spending for the last decade into this. I might add that a voluntary contribution came from one of our observer states as well, our richest observer state by far. They don't want to sign the Human Rights Convention, but they do like spending money. This project was championed behind the scenes by an off-the-books committee headed by a

US Senator. I'm sure you can guess his name."

"I don't follow," said Vicky.

"Your brother in-law has a healthy interest in the unknown, my dear. He's guided you to this device. This is the culmination of the projects of many important men."

"But it's underground. It's – what is it really?"

Nils came closer. "It's interconnected. And capable of making new connections. It learns."

Vicky's eyebrows went up.

"Well for now it's just measuring values, logging bits. We're trying to input our world, but we can only go down to a scale so small. There are always more bits, more detail. What we need is some analog analysis. That's what helps us recognize patterns, but the Vicki doesn't see the forest for the trees. There are more colors that the machine can pick up, but we need to tell it where to draw the boundaries. We need you to define the colors, turn them into usable input. The Vickie has a digital eye that can discern wavelengths, measure the colors. But we need your eyes to make sense of what it's 'seeing'. Once we have a type of key, we can make quick work of the data. Our universe is more simple than it seems, I'm afraid. We've created an accurate recording of our world, Laney. Our goal now is to calculate the code that created it, compress it down to pure math. We want to make an equation out of our world."

Nils went into more detail than Vicky's comprehension of the light spectrum would allow. But she understood completely the intentions of the wayward Secretary General and the subterranean doctor. They claimed a need for understanding, but Vicky recognized the desire that she'd seen in countless iterations. It was a desire not only to know, but to own. Nils and Carl's desperate work was an effort to reduce the universe to something they could scrawl onto a napkin and slip into their pocket, hoping the fire of knowledge wouldn't burn its way through. Vicky's mind had wandered, considering compacting everything she could know into a string, but stood at attention when Nils mentioned Nico.

"I wouldn't trust that mole you're shacking up with by the river. I thought we'd closed up the access from underground rodents, but after your visit, I see that's not so. Remind me to fix that. Nicolas seems to think that chamber below belongs to him too. Most people don't understand our project, I'm certain he wouldn't. Did you know he's only calling himself Arbogast to wring money out of me? His grandmother's supposed house is where the prison nursery will go. He thinks there's some old yellow paper somewhere that says the house belongs to Arbogast so his rat family never changed their names back after the Saint Kell Solidarity in the 40s. He's a liar, an untrustworthy kid, that Nicolas."

"I think the kid is almost 30, Mr. Secretary," said Vicky with a slight blush as she thought proudly of her younger, rattier companion.

"Well, he's a tiny, thieving little man. I have to pay him 600K for that rotten little heap of a house just to tear it down," said Nils, looking Vicky squarely in the eye. He added, "Be wary of people who impede your progress, Laney." But Vicky's eyes didn't center on Nils. They were focused on the periphery, where they clearly detected Nico squatting in the shadows, his finger to his lips.

*

When Vicky emerged through the basement of the castle house she was greeted by candlelight in the round room. Nico was seated cross-legged in the middle, having returned via the tunnels while Nils Winter's chauffeur dropped Vicky off in an impossibly shiny black car.

"Is it true, Nico, that you've stolen someone's identity? What does that even mean, that you're not an Arbogast? Don't you want to know who you really are?"

"And you? Vicky Victoria? That doctor says you are someone else."

"Laney. Yes. Laney Enders was my name. That's not who I am anymore. But I know my family, my roots. They're Victorias. I know the whole mangled tree, back to England, Austria and Germany."

"But that is not you then, you talk only of your adopted family."

"I adopted their past. It's better than the one I was born with. I guess you've just done the same thing, Nico, but for money. I just find it dishonest. You're taking someone else's inheritance. You're stealing.

"Ouri Arbogast, the real one who has his name on the deed of Mamama's house? Well he was a car thief and Jew, just like the car thief Jew that's his father. My family is one of many to save him and his. I don't believe I owe him more than that. They survive on account of us, my people. When the Jews get their property back after the war, and all the residents of Saint Kell find their old names in the *keller*, Mamama keeps the name of Ofira and she gets to keep her rabbits. The minimum, the least he can do, Arbogast can give me his house, that pile of crap next to prison, yes? Best thing that happens to that place is to tear it down. The money is for this place, this house. I will buy it, I will live here legally."

"Then you'll let the light in?" asked Vicky in the candleglow.

"Yes, I'll open the *volets* when it's mine," replied Nico, standing as he spoke.

Vicky gathered he was talking about the hideous, roll-down shutters. "Why do you care anyway? There isn't any real Arbogasts left to claim it. I say it's mine as much as anyone else. I did live there during 18 years."

"You aren't even curious though? To know their names? I mean your family's real name?"

"Why, you afraid we're cousins?" he said with a smile before applying a full-pressure kiss.

"No, I guess I just like mysteries," she said before laying down next to him. He wasn't smoking today and, yet, here he was, talking to her in full sentences. The dim light gave her the courage to ask what she'd been poring over for several nights. "Nico, why do you burn cars? I mean, they belong to people. You're not just breaking things, you're hurting people."

"Insurance probably pay for it. We're not in the *quartier* around the Assembly. People expect stuff around here. Expect fires. You should see St. Sylvestre."

"Who's that?"

"No, St. Sylvestre is New Year. New Year's Eve? It is a parade of burning automobiles in place like this," he said with a mischievous smile, only irking Vicky more.

"But you're intentionally making Saint Kell into an armpit. That's terrible. You're terrible. Aren't you?" She'd been hoping her assumptions about his vehicular arson were wrong.

"How else can someone like me live in a castle by the river?" spat Nico, with mounting defense. The cynicism shone in the narrowing of his eyes. He propped himself up on one elbow and glared at her. "I keep the market in check for my future purchase."

Vicky looked at him critically, both disgusted and intrigued by his selfishness, and wondering if he intended for her to stay in his new home. He threw back a blanket and stood up abruptly. "I work on bus stops too," he said nastily as he walked out, presumably on a quest to break municipal glass.

*

Nico didn't come home the next day or the following night. When he finally came back the day after, he rang the bell of his own front door. Vicky opened it to the smell of stale smoke and unwashed clothes. "Will you come with me?" he pleaded, although Vicky wasn't sure if he'd pronounced any words. The desperation carved into Nico's face implied that he meant it in a larger sense, like he was trying to grab her hand as he jumped off a cliff.

"I will," she replied steadily. There sure was something to be said for saying she was sure about something.

They returned to the place they'd met, Nico's doomed childhood home, awkwardly glued next to the prison wall. He unlocked the front door and held her hand as she walked through.

"This is where the nut from the Assembly want to put the babies."

"The babies? What are you talking about?"

"For prison. He rips this house down for build a nursery."

"I thought he meant a nursery for plants. A greenhouse."

"Nils Winter calls it a human rights issue. Not kosher to separate criminal mommies and babies. So instead of letting the mothers out, they're letting the babies in. The best part is, they think they help. By having babies born prisoners, they helping." Vicky tried to respond, but Nico continued, "Two kids from my school end up in there – only one is released. Every time another Turk or Beur dies in there, they say this was a suicide. There must be awful lot of misery in there, my Mamama say. And with misery come the

121

opportunity." Nico walked over to the dark kitchen and brought a handful of potatoes back. "This is where I work, Vicky. At least until this place goes. Let me show you."

He handed her a potato and her fingers moving over the fine silt made her shiver. She turned it over in her hand, but didn't know what to think. "Do you sell potatoes?"

"I sell very small quantities of very special potato." Nico took the tuber from her and pressed the side with his thumb. A pre-cut tube of potato came out the other side. He turned it to reveal a small cavity, with rolled up euro notes inside. "This arrive in my yard yesterday. I always ask for the money up front."

Vicky looked perplexed, but was obviously amused. "So, what now?"

"Now we fill the order. How much is inside?"

Vicky unrolled the wet, colorful money. "60 euros, no 65," she said as she found a smaller blue 5 euro note in the center of the wad.

"Then we need bigger potato," said Nico, grinning. He grabbed a potato from the bag on the floor and used a metal tube to cut a new core. He then carefully hollowed out a portion of the cylinder. He took a plastic bag from under the sink and pulled out a wrapped plastic pouch. Vicky couldn't see through the many layers of plastic wrap, but she knew what kinds of things came in small packages.

"So you're a drug dealer in addition to being an arsonist and an identity thief?" Her even tone reassured Nico about the things Vicky couldn't say. She'd accepted him that morning when he'd reached out his weathered hand, all of him, and anything she could learn about him now just filled in her sketch of him, adding detail and relief.

They walked outside with the hash potato and Nico's thin, muscular arm tossed it nearly straight up, but with just enough angle to fall back down behind the prison wall. Ten seconds went by, then a pair of anonymous voices shouted, "Merci."

"This is what you wanted me to see? To see if it's too much?"

"No, we just here at the right time today. The product must arrive between 10:10 and 10:20, if no we wait until next day. Mamama set up the planning;

business goes strong for three years now. But, no, you come here so I show you something else. My old room."

"You want to me to see your teddy bear? Doudours?" Vicky spoke playfully as she try to gain points by remembering referencing his stuffed animal form boyhood, but Nico didn't smile.

Nico's tone suddenly became monotone as he spoke, too serious to be excited as he led her down a tight hallway. "I don't understand at first, it take some time. When I hear you talk to Nils Winter the other day, it starts to become clear. When he mention that the Vicki has an eye, artificial eye, I know. That machine under the prison is Dajjal. A beast. The messiah, but fake."

"You think an underground computer is the antichrist?"

"The Dajjal is deceiver. What that machine show you, what it creates, not the truth. No *verité*."

"I don't even understand what it's supposed to create, what it's supposed to even do."

"It creates a false world. Imposter. One that seem real in all ways to observer. But created by man, not by Allah. No, no, not even by man, by machine." Vicky only shook her head as Nico continued and gripped firmly onto her elbow, directing her slowly down the dim wallpapered hallway. "My book says Dajjal need to be thrown into flames. Look, Vicky. I make a machine of my own."

There were wires connecting a laptop computer and an immense, wooden rectangular box, containing more than Vicky cared to know. The resulting apparatus was a frightful marriage of technology and heft.

"It's a bomb, Vicky. Powerful one. It will take down the beast, but I need you to get me to it. They convinced you have some powers to turn it on. I need you make sure it never turn on, never be used. This is why we never find *tauroctonie*; it have not happen yet."

"What is the tauroctony? I think you're lost, Nico. I—"

"No, not lost, Vicky. I never am so sure as now about where I am, why I am here. Tauroctony is Mithras, killing the bull. Same scene in every one of his temple. But the Mithraeum, the room where the Vicki want to come alive, it never had this usual statue. Because Vicki is the bull. You must make it happen."

"Make what happen, Nico? You want me to blow up that machine? Is that all you wanted me for?"

"You are Mithras, Vicky. You're Ubermensch. You're the Superman, not your sister. You need to go to this cave and slay the bull."

*

Dreams came that night, too many to remember. Nightmares that bled into wakefulness. Semiconscious visions that shrunk Nico's bomb down to a vest. Dreams that she was the bull, slain like Saint Victoria. Dreams of her lover standing over her with a sword in hand, surrounded by flaming cars, making her the martyr she'd never asked to be. Then, she's Laney again, playing a piano, the imported Fazioli with the cracked soundboard at Grandma and Grandpa Victoria's house. But there are more notes than her fingers could possibly be playing. She looks to her left and sees Vicky, her 4 year-old twin, shining and smiling as she plays by her side. Turning in the other direction, she sees Ping, her slender fingers tinkling across the tops of the high notes. But next to Ping, like Russian nesting dolls are all the Victoria sisters, Hua, Li-Hua, Meilen and Jade, lined up with hands outstretched over the endless row of keys. Millions of notes play like a rainstorm on the piano as colors churn and condense to form outlines of the round space.

Vicky woke up alone on the cold floor, half off the mattress, but Nico had placed a stocking cap on her head before leaving. She lifted it up as the static electricity pulled her hair and a rush of cold poured in. She pulled the cap back down and started to get dressed. She had to pay someone a visit.

*

Wooden beams arched up in a 1960s fashion that made the Assembly look like a church. A large front desk with 3 uniformed agents asked for her ID and who she was visiting. "The Secretary General, Nils Winter. He invited me, he just didn't know I was coming today."

The agents eyed each other suspiciously and one finally spoke up. "Nils Winter is no longer the Secretary General. His second term ended more than a decade ago." Vicky assumed they were trying to screen out crazed people from the street showing up in unwashed clothes and ridiculous stocking caps.

"But he told me to come here. He came to see me, actually, in St. Kell."

The two agents look at each other again, this time amused. "Yeah, he never gets tired of this place. He still does work here, but he's now the Swedish Deputy Permanent Representative to the Assembly. There are no meetings today, but his Residence is just down the street from here. I can give you the address. He always likes to see contractors from the St. Kell project personally."

Vicky's anger built as she approached the frilly cube that was the Swedish Permanent Representation. She knew he hadn't gotten it wrong; he'd specifically asked her to come to the Assembly. She imagined how everyone saw her, a tool to use for their own devices. All their passions and plans funneled through the girl from the dark. Vicky was sure Nils was making her go on a chase; convincing herself through her actions that she needed to find him. Surprisingly, it happened exactly as planned and by the time she reached the Representation, she was more than eager to see Mr. Winter again.

She walked up the front steps and banged on a ridiculously tall door. Nils Winter opened the front door himself and smiled, making his tiny blue eyes shrink even more. He looked so much older without his navy blue suit, clad in dark jeans and a polo shirt that displayed a desire for anonymity.

"Deputy?" said Vicky with raised eyebrows.

"Well, yes, I suppose I am a Deputy. Aren't we all really? But the particulars of this handsome title allowed me to remain in Strasbourg after my retirement. I'm not that keen on heading north again. It's too cold. Speaking of cold, come in before all my heat gets sucked out into the wind. Wonky radiators in these old buildings. Nice hat, by the way. Are you some kind of revolutionary?"

"I—what do you mean? It's just to keep my head warm. It was a gift, I guess."

"A gift? That's a rather strange one. Look at how it falls forward on your head. It looks like the Kàffeewärmer."

"Ummm—"

"Well, come in! If we're going to talk revolution, at least let it be over tea."

Vicky followed the tall, handsome old man as he barreled through a great hall with a curved staircase and into a room decorated with conspicuous gold trim. "Could it be something stronger?" she ventured. Nils turned around and winked, then snapped his fingers and left her at an ornately carved table.

He returned nearly ten minutes later with two paper cups, placing one in front of Vicky. She took a sip. She smiled as the drink burned its way down her throat, tracing a line to her stomach. "That's considerably stronger than tea, Nils."

"This is one of my old Canadian intern's recipes. Caribou. I'm glad you like it. So, what were we discussing? The revolution! Yes, your *bonnet rouge*. Let's go for a walk, Laney. Some stories require illustration."

A short stroll down uneven cobblestones brought them to the foot of the cathedral. Vicky wondered if it was the church that was drawing her back and not Nils. She'd stayed right here with Suresh not long ago, but it seemed like a century now. "Like the one in Paris, this one's also called Notre Dame. Notre Dame de Strasbourg. I thought you could do the Doctor a favor here, you know, light a candle?" Vicky looked at Nils' light blue eyes and tried to read what sort of captor he was; the Doctor was clearly not able to leave the prison like a normal worker, yet Nils obviously had compassion for him.

"What about my hat, Nils?"

"That particular type of cap is a symbol of the French Revolution, among other things. I believe your US Senate even uses it in their seal. Perhaps Mr. Vickie would know about that. Anyway, here, the hat is the symbol of freedom, and perhaps freedom gone too far. See, the revolutionaries were inclined to remove any signs of religion or inequality from their landscape, but they got a bit overzealous in their efforts. They wanted a simple world, one that was categorical and flat. They changed the months, the days, even the hours."

"Why change the months?"

"They wanted to scrub off the taint of any gods. May had been named for the goddess Maya so it became Floréal, for the flowers. No one ever really knew what day or what time it was, just floating through the ether they were. And what a revolution it was! They started over with year one. Because they had ten fingers, they said everything should be based on tens. Ten hours, ten months, ten years. But the moon doesn't have ten fingers so it wasn't brilliantly on-board with the plan. Anyway, they also wanted to lob the top off Notre Dame de Strasbourg."

Vicky craned her head straight back to look up the facade of the 800-year-old sandstone cathedral. It was dizzying in its height and complexity, but also strangely fitted with only one spire.

"They wanted to decapitate it, remove any reference to religion or inequality, take off the one spire that she had. I suppose that would have made her symmetrical anyway: A bit of an odd duck as churches go, isn't she? Well, a local locksmith was the voice of reason – and he lived right there." Nils swung around and pointed to a building on the square. "To get his message across, he had to use the symbols of the revolution. He fashioned a giant tin hat and painted it red to look like the one those fools wore in the name of equality. Just like you, the Cathedral of Strasbourg wore a giant red Phrygian cap. You could see it all the way from Germany on a clear day. The church wore that hat for 8 years and was saved from destruction. So your 'gift' is quite a commanding piece of headgear."

Vicky removed the hat once again and turned it around in her hands, feeling the tug of two men who craved too much commitment from her. It suddenly seemed easier to be repeatedly abandoned; at least there was no choice involved. She considered her words carefully, evaluating in real time whether she was betraying Nico as the piano music from her dream kept playing in the background of her thoughts. "I think the person who gave me this thinks I'm something I'm not. He thinks I'm important, like you do, but in a different way. Nils, I'm afraid the project may be in jeopardy because of his...passion."

"I have a feeling you're referring to Mr. Arbogast? I wouldn't think him capable of much, Laney, he's a vagrant with mental issues. But I appreciate your concern. Your help will move us to the next phase and we'll be out of the woods, as they say. Nothing can stop true knowledge from shining through." He smiled and sipped his Caribou from the now dented paper cup as a strong wind whipped around his scalp at the base of the church. It was difficult to tell where the current of air stopped and his hair started. "Shall we go inside? Do your duty?"

Once they were inside, Nils motioned to a modern-looking stained-glass window. "Look right up there. That's a gift from my Assembly after the worst of the wars. The bombs pulled the original glass clear out with the wind so the Assembly gave the city this gift. See the top? No logic, there, no ten, orderly stars. We even had ten member states at the beginning. It would have made perfect sense. But we put twelve."

"Why twelve?"

"Because we were following our leaders, Vicky. Our past. Even when we don't know why, we still want to commemorate something. Twelve disciples, twelve months, twelve signs of the zodiac."

"The twelve knights of the round table?"

"How far back do you want to go? I raise you twelve Olympians. Twelve Titans! We don't know why, but we make sure to preserve things that seem important. Our project is part of that."

"Part of what?"

"Well, just like for this church window dame, we're not completely sure yet. She's the secular symbol of Europe, although no one knows what she represents yet with her fancy headdress. People like symbols, even if they don't know what they symbolize. Even if they mean different things to different people."

"You're a great leader, Nils. You'll make this project happen…Whatever it is you're trying to do."

"Laney, I can't make anything happen any more than you. But I can keep going forward. I'm getting old and I don't know what I believe, where I can go. But leaders aren't blazing trails, cutting through vines to choose the path. They're just driving on tracks that are already in place, dragging you with them. So if I'm a great leader, all I can do is go forward, and hopefully carry some souls with me along the way." He half-smiled as he looked at Vicky for a long minute. "Shall we light that candle now for dear dad?"

They emerged from the Cathedral as Nils chattered about the great astronomical clock inside, drawing parallels with astral bodies and days of the week, finishing by mentioning that he was ravenous. They crossed the cathedral square and he paused to point up at a cannon shell embedded into the corner of a hotel. "That was a gift from the Kaiser," Nils said with a wink and then walked into a courtyard with a dining area. Vicky started for a table, but Nils took her elbow and motioned to a stairway leading down.

They dipped underground into a cave-turned-restaurant.

The restaurant was vast with vaulted ceilings and several hidden corners. They followed an aproned employee down and around, then back up and down again to a room that looked like a smaller version of the room with the Vicki. A grand piano took up nearly half the space and the rest was crammed with tables for two, although Nils and Vicky were the only ones present and each felt like they had been invited by the other.

Fully accustomed to meeting Nils underground, Vicky drew on her midnight learning from hours ago. The music in her head was louder now in the presence of the piano and she tossed an analogy on the table as they peeled off coats. Tilting her head toward the piano she asked, "Nils, do you play?"

"Why's that? Are you afraid that lovely white instrument over there is neglected? You may be right. Yes, I reckon I play, but played may be more accurate. Would you like me to kick off some of the dust?" He wore an amused look on his face and stepped toward the piano to press a key. The single key he pressed played perfectly into the music swirling around her brain, completing an ethereal chord.

"Nils, I think we need to work fast, work differently. Let's speed things up. Accelerate the project. You call a C note a *do* right? Do, re, mi?"

"I don't follow, Laney," said Nils, but his expression could not contain the glee that Vicky was somehow on board with his vision.

Vicky continued, "If you see sheet music and you try to tell someone what note to play, well, if they don't speak your language, they don't know what you mean. I don't know which note is a *mi*, Nils. We use the alphabet for notes in America."

"So you show them the music then? They read the notes in their language," said Nils as he tried to sound non-committal, but brimmed with excitement.

"No, Nils, the sheet music is the world around us. We don't need your code for that. We can already see it, we just don't know how to read it, translate it."

"Whatever do you suggest, my dear?" he said as he furtively pulled a flask out and added more burn to their drinks. How this man could continually combine whiskey and wine was beyond her, but Vicky sipped the stripped-down Caribou of the restaurant nonetheless.

Setting down her glass, she continued. "We need to play the music. Not just learn the equation or the program, but run it. Go live."

"You mean you want to run a simulation of our world? Our universe? You'll have to speak to Andrei about that. He holds the keys to that particular conundrum of a castle."

"Who is Andrei?"

"My most trusted Ambassador and very good friend. We share an unquenchable thirst for order and meaning."

"Where is he?" asked Vicky, raising her glass again.

"Oh, he's dead. He had a heart attack back home in Russia." Nils gazed evenly over Vicky's shoulder in suddenly distracted thought.

Both sat quietly for a moment, then he dug around in his wallet and pulled out a folded postcard, its texture worn to near fabric after riding around Nils' pocket for what must have been a long time. He unfolded the card and placed it on the table in front of Vicky. "This is the last time I heard from Andrei. He took his family on a road trip for two days to go see this thing. Read it."

There was a picture of a wooden church set against a blue sky.

Vicky turned the card over:

> *Nils,*
> *Master Nestor built this church without nails. He used nothing but an axe. When he was done, he threw his axe into Lake Onega so that there would never be one like it.*
> *Yours faithfully,*

Andrei

"He didn't believe a true creator would make his code open-source. You see, we embarked on a journey of discovery. A decades-long project that Andrei never got to finish. A project to reveal what is going on, what made us and how. But think also about the why. We were not always in agreement about the why. Andrei believed that we could not create, only observe. I suppose it's a good thing too. Doctor Enders got very close once. He thought he had the formula, the one that would iterate and tessellate and copy and turn, one that would create the seemingly endless place we know as home. But it wasn't right. There were problems. It was close, but it wasn't close enough. It was a bit like rounding pi down to 3."

"So? What happened?"

"Well, he lost part of himself in it, to be honest. He ended it up scrapping it. Started over. He couldn't keep zooming. He kept going further and further down, there was just no end in sight. We wanted you to help with that issue. Not to make a substandard copy of our universe, Laney."

"And what if we're already in a copy? Would we even know if we're in whatever he turned on? Wouldn't we have the right to do the same? If someone created us and made us capable of creation, aren't we allowed? Even if we're a photocopy?"

"Well, I don't know about you, but I feel quite real. I like to think I'm in the original version of whatever this is."

"Of course you do, Nils. That's the point. If the Vicki is strong enough to learn the code, it's strong enough to play it back."

"*Flammekueche!*" Vicky realized this last word was meant for a waiter behind her by the waving motion of Nils' right hand. With no further explanation to what he had just ordered, Mr. Winter continued.

"Laney, your generation is not accustomed to patience. To tell you the truth, mine isn't either. I suppose your simulation would create a here and now reality with the same baggage of the past to try to actually change things. There's more than grandparents meeting and unmissed trains though. There's all of humanity to consider. We humans, for all our supposed knowledge, were here for millennia before we could even speak. Can you quite imagine that in your lightly peppered youth?"

His voice got louder as he reached across the table to pound his index finger on her empty plate. His blue eyes caught fire like pilot lights that had finally been given more gas. "I bet you can convince yourself that I'm not even here, Laney. That I'm someone you've constructed. That you've already figured it all out, that this is your game and you've already saved the princess a billion times over. Without a challenge, without a fight, you're right to assume that infinite existence gets pretty boring. So you're reinventing yourself, cheating at Solitaire, playing the role of the battered some such or other to make your points in this flittering, fleeting, artificial existence count more. Well, don't believe I haven't felt the same, Laney Enders! Felt that everyone—the lovers, the leavers and all the passersby—they're the same person. The same old you ground up and spit out to teach you something, to make you feel something!"

Vicky tried to interject, but Nils was on a roll. "And you know what they say about women looking for their fathers? I don't buy it. In your world, which father is that Nico character to you, Carl or Lothaire? You're not looking for your father, you're all just looking for someone who mirrors yourself back. The gestures, the looks, the speech of a father are the same traits he's passed on to you. You're already reflecting yourself in your perception of your whole world. We're all narcissists, I get it. And so do you, Laney! But if you can feel that and I can feel that, then aren't we meant to wait things out and see how the game goes rather than rebooting as soon as we start to understand? These things we're dealing with, these selfish desires to create, aren't they too dangerous?"

Tired from his tirade, Nils did a polite version of slumping into his chair.

"Perhaps you're right about plugging it in," said Vicky.

"Funny, I was just thinking the opposite," replied Nils, with the even stare of a partner in crime. "After all, I'm a very curious person." It appeared that his exhausting rebuke had been meant to convince himself more than Vicky.

"If it's true that we're all the same, that we're all you or all me, what would happen if I tried to take someone with?" asked Vicky.

"In the simulation? The created world? Why? Is Nico so dark that he's sucked you in? Your twin black hole?"

"I want to take him to the next place, have more time to get to know him. I thought I was meant to be alone. No matter what, I've always ended up alone. I've woken up a thousand times, knowing someone should be there next to me. Knowing there's someone out there; that it's not just me. When I met Nico, I didn't feel it anymore, feel his absence. Because he was there. Most people can't see it, see what they're leaving. They just envision themselves going forward, without realizing they're leaving others behind. Leaving me behind. I don't want to do that, Nils. I don't just want to end with Nico. I want to start with him. I want to keep him."

"But he's nothing, Laney. Even you just said it. He's no one. He's just a fraction of the greater you. You can't keep him separate because he's a building block of who you are. Keeping him as this entity, this self, could only produce an error. He'll always be with you, but in a different way. He'll fold back in."

"No, I want to keep him how he is, the exact configuration. I want him just the way he is."

"You're starting to sound like Billy Joel. Ah, our feast has arrived. Have a piece of *tarte flambée* and think it over. I'd like to afford you the leadership role on this one, Laney. I'll follow you wherever your track takes you, but you may want to talk to the sister first. Marianne Topoglu. She has power of attorney for Nicolas and knows more than I do about his, how shall we say, stability. She's been working on the Niedergass house settlement with me, the one I have to buy from Nicolas to complete my nursery. I'll give you her number and I'm sure she'd be more than thankful to have news of her brother. From what I gather, they don't speak much. And by not much, I mean not at all."

Vicky drew her attention back to the *tarte flambée*, a hot rectangular flatbread that sat steaming before them on a wooden paddle, its sprinkling of bacon glistening back at her. "I'm a vegetarian, Nils."

"By choice?" he replied with a smile.

"By marriage," she returned as Nils raised both brows.

"Yes, Carlos mentioned that you started your *séjour* in St. Kell with another beau. May I ask why you're lobbying to bring Nicolas on this doomed journey and not your husband?" He grabbed a slice of the tarte and folded it, stuffing a corner into his mouth. Vicky had never imagined the former Secretary General of the Assembly of Europe eating with his hands. Her eyes widened as he began licking his fingers.

"My husband moved to India without me. We're not divorced, just…" But she couldn't find a word for this particular form of abandonment.

"I believe they call it 'estranged,' Laney. And I'm sorry to hear it. Perhaps, as a gesture of your moving on, you could estrange yourself from your relationship with vegetarianism to try this delicious *flammekueche*."

Vicky thought briefly about the dietary borrowings from the men in her life. Suresh called beef sacred and Nico called pork dirty. She decided that for this moment, she'd let herself be pulled into the gravity of yet another man, a fairly recent addition to her repertoire, and picked up a slice of the divine from the depths of a Strasbourg cellar.

THE AMERICAN
(2011)

Marianne picked up the phone on the first ring, like she'd been waiting for Vicky's call.

"You're American?" she asked right away.

"Yes, does that matter?" asked Vicky.

"It does, but I'm not entirely sure why."

Vicky contemplated why she'd even called. She'd chosen Nico to continue whatever life this was, by her side. Nothing would sway her at this point. But Marianne seemed intent on answering questions that no one asked.

"You Americans are eternally trying to find where you came from, discover your past. But in France, we've lived with ours for thousands of years, we can't escape it. When we know too much, we refrain from talking about it. And if we don't talk about it for long enough, we start to forget. The next generation doesn't find it mysterious or captivating. Just done. Over. They want to live in the now. We all want to live our lives without the burden of our ancestors' follies."

Vicky cut in. "You mean the Arbogasts, right? Or whatever your family was, whoever they were? Nico doesn't seem to even know."

"So, this I can tell you. He does know, by the way. My brother knows more than he lets on. Our grandmother, we called her Mamama, she was born, lived and died Ofira Arbogast. That's all she ever was. There's no further mystery to discover, no hidden roots to dig up. Ours was the family that St. Kell saved. We were the helpless, the family spawned from thieves. My great grandfather stole a car from Kaiser Wilhelm in 1919 and that's how we came to St. Kell. To hide. It was outside of the walls of the city back then."

Vicky interrupted again to insert the result of her own research to the matter. "I thought Lanvin was arrested in Paris. I found an article in the archives of the New York Times."

"That was so the French authorities could save face. Lanvin was some other guy they wanted for some other indiscretion so they pinned it on him. They never recovered the car though. I think it did end up in St. Kell somewhere, probably with my great-grandfather behind the wheel…

"The thing is, Nico is obsessed with too much from the past. There were these aniconic patterns that he found in a Muslim mosque, patterns that he thought described the world. It started as a simple classic pattern, but to him it became building blocks for a greater order or something. He got lost in those tiles, those thoughts."

"Well, his religion seems very important to him. I think it's normal to get lost in what you believe in."

Marianne let out an audible sigh. "That's just it though. It's not his religion. I converted before I married and I know what I believe. Nico didn't convert, he doesn't go to mosque, he just picks and chooses whatever he wants from Islam, whatever he thinks he understands."

"Well, he's more of an Islamic scholar then. I admire his dedication, even if it is unconventional."

"The term 'Islamic Scholar' is an oxymoron, Ms. Victoria. To study the teachings is to believe, to know. It's not about learning. My brother denies that he's from the tribe of Israel and that's the only reason he tries for understanding with Islam. He doesn't realize he's living and breathing the very tenant of Judaism, the persistent doubt. I'm a believer in Allah, in Muhammad's teaching, peace be upon him. But Nico has too many questions. He's still wandering through the desert and it makes him dangerous."

Vicky paused before speaking. "This doesn't change anything for me. He's an incredible person, Marianne. This doesn't make him dangerous, it makes him alive. I've never felt complete like I do with him. I met your brother, maybe two months ago? But I've known him for much longer, I don't know how to explain it."

"Ms. Victoria, Nico wants to be a savior, or a martyr, something with more meaning to him than a sheltered soul. Maybe he's found a kindred spirit in you, someone who needs validation too. He's invented a pattern, a complexity, that isn't there. You need to be extremely careful with him. Nico's been off the radar for the last year. He's supposed to be at his assigned site. The thing is, it's a court order; he's a criminal as long as he's at large. His case worker there says he hasn't checked in. The order could be enforced if he doesn't comply. He could go to prison, Ms. Victoria." Vicky couldn't help smiling at the thought of such a minor move to the other side of the wall as Marianne continued.

"He sent my husband a disturbing message a few days ago. He was referencing an *ayah* from Surah al-Baqarah, one that talks about going from darkness into the light. I'm sure you're not familiar, but al-Baqarah is the chapter of the Koran about slaughtering a cow. I don't know what he means, Ms. Victoria, but part of it makes more sense to me now. He said he has a new American to slay the bull. I don't know what he's gotten you into, but it's very important that he sees his case worker at Berges de l'Ain. Even if he's not living there, you must understand that Nico has serious problems."

"What's Berges de l'Ain?" Vicky couldn't help asking.

"That's where they put someone like my brother who has nowhere else to go. He went there after getting in trouble, after a few weeks on the street. It was about that damned car. He said my husband was a thief. Because he thinks stealing that car is in his blood somehow, that the responsibility is his. But instead he calls Mehmet a thief, just to cleanse himself."

"What does he think Mehmet stole?"

It took a few seconds of empty space for her to respond. "Mehmet was really into cars when he was a boy. He collected about 50 die-cast models. When Nico told him about the Mercedes—that's the car that was stolen— he thinks that Mehmet found the car before him and stole the engine."

"Why would he do that?"

"To sell, I guess. It was rare and valuable, some sort of special system. I don't know, Mehmet knows what it is, but he didn't take it. He's never even seen the car. He doesn't believe it even exists. Nico thinks he snuck underground somehow, found the car and removed the whole engine to sell on the black market. As a little kid. I mean, this is the kind of person you're dealing with, Miss. He thinks my husband betrayed him. Nico…he took a dull axe to Mehmet's hand one day. For punishment. He almost lost it, lost his hand. Maybe it would have been better if he did. After four surgeries, he still can't move most of the fingers on his left hand. He had to stop playing guitar. He nearly lost his job because he practically lived at the clinic. I'm sorry, I've said too much, but you should really just stay away from him. They only let him off because Mehmet wouldn't press charges. They sent Nicolas to Berges de l'Ain and he's supposed to follow the program. Change his colors. You need to help him get back there, Ms. Victoria. It's the best for both of you, you need to believe me. You need to leave him there."

*

Something carried Vicky through another week. She felt quartered, tied and ready to be pulled in too many directions as soon as the horses were spooked. Seven days after what had already seemed like the end of time, she was next to the Vicki, another adopted sister she would try to understand. Nico was with her, so were Nils and Carl. The sum of their parts made her feel whole enough to mask the panic reflecting off the walls of the dungeon Nico called the Unterkeller. The false Dr. Enders, whose name now seemed irrelevant, explained the process, the sedation and the moment they'd power up the Vicki to do something heavy, although no one was quite sure what it was.

Nils pulled a small rectangle from his pocket, then passed it to Nico. For all his disdain of the young man, he pressed it tenderly into his hand, like a father would palm a son his pocket money. Nico warily unfolded the paper next to Vicky as they sat on the floor of the underground shrine to the universe. There was a pen and ink drawing of some type of apparatus on it that Vicky didn't recognize, but Nils' words cast light onto the page.

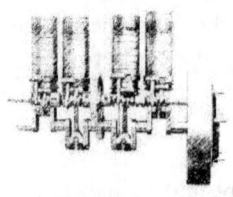

"I'm the one who took this from your family, Nico. It's the American; I made this sketch when I first laid eyes on it. See, we found the Kaiser's car when excavating for our prison. Your grandmother came to see me when we started digging; she knew what we would find and she wanted to make a deal. She needed to forget what her father had done and she longed to keep her home in St. Kell, even if it meant living next to my prison. The house did belong to her, to the Arbogasts, but she had nothing to prove it, no papers. Ofira agreed to give me this motor—the American—to keep her house. It was a beautiful piece of equipment, a sleeve-valve engine created by Charles Knight. He was from the States, hence the name. The American was what made the Kaiser's Mercedes purr. That's what your great grandfather wanted; that's what he stole. I got 200,000 francs for it in the eighties, but it was worth more than that. I really should have saved it.

"Well, Ofira gave us permission to wall off her sub-basement and use the site. Your grandmother gave us rights to expand our property below, but she also transferred the home into a trust that I own. I guess it was a bit of a deception on my part. But we had a deal. As long as she was alive the house would be hers to live in. When she passed, it would become property of the prison. I know that you always thought you would get something for it, but what you didn't realize is that I already own it. I don't have to give you a penny for what's already mine. That's why your sister has been struggling with the paperwork for so long, Nico. It will never be yours. But I know that old car is still parked on the other side of that wall, Nico, less its beating heart. Less the engine, but still there, smiting a dead Kaiser for your forefathers. It will soon be buried in dirt for the foundations of my nursery. For what it's worth, I want you to understand that I know who you truly are. I know what I've taken from you is not just. I'm prepared to finance the white house on the river for you if you decide that's your destiny. From my own pocket, Nico. You need to be sure that this is how you want to continue, with this relative stranger into the unknown. You need to know that you have an alternative, that you have a home. I apologize that I tried so long to take that away from you. But it was all for this. For this project, Nicolas Arbogast. You can still back out. This machine was meant for Laney, not for you."

Nico took Vicky's hand in his, still unaccustomed to hearing her former name. His palm was rough and calloused, both dry and warm to the touch. "I made my choice," he said, although it seemed to be directed at the machine more than the man. Vicky's body grew immobile from the sedative Carl Enders had given to both for the process, but she positioned her hand in Nico's, weaving her fingers into his so that the two would remain clasped, even in the absence of muscular will. To let go of him now would be a life without purpose.

Her body was still, but her mind began racing in messy orbits around a central truth. Vicky suddenly knew that the bomb was no longer in Nico's childhood bedroom. She knew why he burned cars as confidently as she knew what was slowly catching fire on the other side of the wall, readying for a spectacular explosion. He had practiced this, infused it with more meaning each time he lit a match. The burning would turn to melting and increase the potential energy until it could no longer be contained by the 1915 Mercedes Knight. The wall would blow loudly enough to destroy ears before they could detect the soundwaves of the explosion. The Vicki and the determined force of curiosity in the Unterkeller would cease to exist. The Vicki's lights were blinking methodically and the heaviness of her eyelids couldn't block the pattern of light. Nico was too late. The machine was already on.

III. Strings

RONNONGWETONWANCA

It's cold. Much too cold to step out of the stalled tram and into the blowing wind of February in Saint Paul. She's been tasked with transporting a child, her twin sister's kid in fact, to the dentist. Apparently the boy has an extra tooth that two dentists and one oral hygienist have already tried to remove, to no avail. The boy is determined to kick at inappropriate intervals when his mother is present, so a third party, a caring but distant aunt, has been chosen as better suited to the task.

A rumor ripples through the tram that the jolt they'd all felt before stopping was the impact of the train with a body. Who would try to end it all by hurling himself at a hunkering tram was lost on Laney. She tried to imagine his face, his name. Imagine how someone could do such a thing.

A tug at her sleeve reminds her of the wide-eyed panic at her side. The strange little boy with the mouth too full of teeth is terrified. She pulls out her phone and steps out of the tram, his hot moist hand in hers at Victoria Street Station. "Isn't that fitting? This stop is named after your mom. Come, we need to call the dentist."

The sounds of the sidewalk chatter and crunching snow are scarcely quieter than the foggy panic within the stationary tram. By the time the Dr. V answers in his musical tone, she is shouting and covering her exposed ear. "Yes, we're on our way, but what? Excuse me, I can't hear you. I'm sorry, the tram is stalled. My nephew and I will be late." Her breath dissipates in a cloud and she looks back to the frightened child who will soon have another large rubber gloved hand in his face, cutting furiously at the roof of his mouth while he screams uselessly, out of range of his protective brothers in the suburbs.

She steals a glance at the front of the train, making sure the boy is facing the other way. Emergency workers are carrying off a long, large body that is too twisted to come back to life. She doesn't see his face, but she catches a glimpse of the soles of his shoes. They're worn thin by someone who's known either great hardship or great passion, walking with purpose for centuries, since before shoes existed. She decides to give the dead man a name.

"Let's go sit in the warm train until it's ready to move again. It's too far to walk. Come, I'll tell you a story." Laney presses the button to slide open the tram door and locates an empty seat. The boy doesn't know he's been the one holding her up.

The Last Ronnongwetowanca (10,000 BCE)

The great Ni-k'o is a giant and he is dying. Only the shaman could save him now, but Ni-k'o is himself the shaman. The medicine man cannot save himself if he wants to be remembered by the smaller people around him. He must die and push away for the momentum to pull him back.

Ni-k'o has a great, powerful head, with three markings so that all will recognize him long after he is gone. He wears all the colors of the universe on the side of his head, mixed into a stripe of white, the wind in his hair. There's a crack in the center of his forehead. It's healed over, but still light shines through. He can see without his eyes. He has more teeth than all the small-boned people to make them believe he will be here longer, to remind them that he will need to eat when he is reborn again and again.

Ni-k'o is dying and he sends his children to the new world so they can call it old. They will wind their fingers around knotted strings and tell tales as tall as the giant. They will run on hills that are their father, then leave with the setting sun. His body will be built up to a mound, his giant frame growing larger, then weathered down by the wind and rebuilt a thousand times. The ground is now Ni-k'o and Ni-k'o is now the ground. When his ancestors return, they will see the ground is breathing.

La-n'i has carried the baskets of dirt with her sisters to bury her beloved shaman. High and proud, Ni-k'o grows taller and wider. He will rise up so the red people can brace their feet a thousand moons later on his great mound. They will not know him, but they will see him in the silver flying off Mni-Tonka. He is scattered now and giving life to more souls than the lights in the sky. La-n'i carries hope in her belly, over the

144

great river Ma'xe-e'ometaa'e on a grapevine that will snap behind her, leaving her sisters to build Ni-k'o higher until she can return.

The people will forget him, but they will find their way back by the rising sun. They will come to the old and call it new, long after Ni-k'o is buried in the mound. They will touch the waters of Mni-Tonka and know they are home.

One day, a daughter of a daughter of La-n'i's thousand daughters back will have three sons. One will be born with the wind in his hair. The second will cut an eye on his forehead and see into souls. The third will have a tooth where others have none. They will come back to walk on the hills of Ni-k'o. They will wind ancient strings around their fingers and they will know they are home.

QUIPU

There are babies burning in her belly, two of them, being constantly infused with the fantastic chemical fear that comes with abstract guilt. Would the babies call someone "mother" or float along isobars as she had done, foster to foster ad infinitum?

Her apocrine terror leaks into the courthouse. They can literally smell her fear. Should she have called Victoire for the hearing? She has no jurisdiction beyond Quatchik County, and certainly not across the ocean from her home to France. But Laney feels something like love for the woman who has come, unrequested, to her rescue several times. She would be able to explain things, pare everything terrible down to an administrative error.

It had been Victoire that had placed her here, at an internship within the Assembly of Europe four months prior. Victoire who had determined that living as a heroin heroine under a bridge was indeed no life at all and *wasn't she a bit old for these shenanigans anyway?* She had called around her old contacts in the Observer State offices to place Laney as far as possible from anything she had known. Victoire knew the Assembly, where she had interned at the Canadian Chancery and carved out a following for Caribou among euro-diplomats. She could find a place for anyone; she had found a place for Laney. But, alas, Laney will not call Victoire now. She would only be a disappointment to the poor woman.

All she knows is that she has no one to go home to. That Maître Topoglu is doing all he can to get her into an experimental nursery wing of the St. Kell Prison. That her new home will now be beating as two hearts deep within her to the rhythm of an unseen drum.

Nicky won't come to see her, this she knows. He'll forget her name, just like he did in front of the ethics panel from the Russian Federation. He probably already has. He'll forget how hard he pulled her hair as she bent over the Norwegian delegation's coats in the cloakroom. Her business casual heels had provided little friction for the thrusting; they were only meant to click and clack across mosaic tiling like horse shoes for a geisha.

Even as the head of the bioethics programme at the Assembly, with an m and an e to show solidarity against American imperialism, he'll never know the ins and out of paternal biology and how quickly one can conceive at the edge of 36, when ovulation becomes a desperate, spontaneous necessity.

No, Nicky the Programme Manager with hairy chest and a golden anchor charm worn around his neck, won't come to see her or send her flowers. He's from such humble roots, a farm boy with ambition. He surely won't testify that she didn't do whatever it is that one supposes she has done. He won't mind that she's going to prison, that she's leaving this world. Perhaps he'll live another two months, at which point he'll be telling jokes that make his entourage erupt in such laughter that an aide in the back will crack a hyena peal. The laughter will be so sonorously comical as to accelerate Nicky's heart and make him lean on a railing two stories up and quaking with glee. The railing will have been installed by a nepotistic contract employing a Romanian cousin, but it will not support the transformation of energies and prevent the free fall of Nicky, sending him to his death below.

Perhaps.

But back to now. What is it now, exactly, that she has done? Visions, glimpses come back, but they are trails she can't follow. In her mind, Nicky is already dead again, an object of his own folly. An accident of his own devices. She sees him there, plunging in slow motion, through the shabbily-constructed railing, through the air, through the veneer layer of tile to the powdery substance that flies up from the cracks in the floor.

> Hide the body.
> Clean the scene.
> Crouch in the bushes when lights drive by.
> The keycard. Shit, the keycard.

So maybe Victoire wouldn't be able to call this an administrative error after all. Nicky, the farm boy who raised rabbits with his grandma in a suburb, would he help? No, she's been through this. Nicky is here. Nicky is not here. Where the fuck is Nicky the Programme Manager when I need him?

She's not wearing an orange jumpsuit like her incarcerated sibling in America. Her clothes look like clothes. But she hasn't yet been approved for elastic in her underpants. Suicide risk they say, but Maître Topoglu is working on that.

The prison chaplain comes at random hours and seems an odd fit: a burly Indian who she doesn't yet know can sing. *Not enough French Catholic priests* he'd said. They're so happy I'm here. She's thankful for an English speaker amid the riotous shouting that is now her life. He takes her into his office once a week. *It's important to remember, to record.* But, what does he mean? *Ancient Mesoamericans wrote their history on a series of strings. They kept records in knots, hundreds of strings, all across a continent; but with no key. No one knows what it means. But at least they left a trace. At least they told a story.*

They're back in a courtroom and Maître Topoglu is arguing now, clothed in the pomp of a black and white smock. "Your honor, she doesn't understand what she's done. She thinks he's still alive. Laney Enders doesn't believe she's murdered Mr. Arbogast. She doesn't remember pushing him in front of 200 witnesses. Doesn't remember mopping his blood and dragging the body in front of fainting dignitaries. She's living a delusion, your honor. Maximum security is not necessary, however consistent medication is."

Her mind wanders to the chaplain and his portrait of the woman with stars around her head. She sits above his desk like a watchman. She's the same woman who hangs in the courthouse, Europe presiding over the justice system. "What does it mean?" she'd asked. "What's she for?"

What had the chaplain said? What had carried some truth through all the details of this hearing? His voice had come through like a tale from a period of more understanding. *And there appeared a great wonder in heaven; a woman clothed with the sun, and the moon under her feet, and upon her head a crown of twelve stars.*

"But what does it mean?" she'd asked, she was sure of it. Sure she'd asked. *You can call it Revelation or you can call it Apocalypse. Verse 12:1. But you need to call it something. Carry it through. Tell a story.*

She knows now as Topoglu gestures toward her blank face, reiterating arguments of innocence that no one will share. She knows she'll hold those two things in her belly like the dollies she never had, wondering if madness runs in the family like twins. Hold them in her nursery cell built right over the ruins of Nicky's rabbit farm. Maybe she'll ask the chaplain for white ribbons to tie in their baby-fine hair. And what kind of stories will she read them in prison?

Clip clop, go the business casual heels.
Swish swish, go the key cards.
It's a new day at the farm.

She lies half-awake the day after the preliminary hearing. The actual trial won't be for months and she already can't sleep at night. She's trying to remember the words of the chaplain, repeating what he's said as though it will make more sense, when a commotion arrives down the corridor. Visitors on a press mission from the Assembly stream by her cell. They're taking photos and scribbling notes until Nils Winter, the Secretary General and de facto Prison Warden himself has somehow commanded the opening of her cell and is now uncomfortably poised on her cot. He motions the photographers away and signals to his assistant, "Marten, I need a moment. No notes please." Then he turns his attention to Laney. "What did you say about that chaplain, Miss? I don't recall there being a chaplain at this site."

"He calls himself Aunt Vicky. Strange, I know, for such a burly man."

"Yes, I thought that's what you said. I have an Aunt Vicky too," he says now hushing his voice, his cornflower eyes trained on hers. He's close to her ear now and smells like maple syrup. "She's the strangest thing in the world. Well, perhaps not much stranger than telling a murderer in my prison about her." He hesitates without taking his eyes off hers, running a million tiny calculations to determine if he should continue. "My Aunt Vicky is an animal, a fox. She glows blue at night and is terrible at keeping secrets. She's trying to give the universe away, a half dream at a time. Does that sound like your chaplain, Miss…"

"Enders. Laney Enders, prisoner 6601. No, the chaplain is a person, not a fox. He looks like a person anyway, and his voice is like a song."

"Miss Enders, I'm inclined to believe Aunt Vicky takes many forms, but carries the same message. In fact, I think I would be more surprised if you said she was your actual aunt and not a large Catholic prison chaplain from the Indian subcontinent. You see, my messenger, in all her florescent glory, let on that her form is dependent on her audience's experiences from the last, um, how shall we define it…life. I remember this precisely because it

150

was the information I was meant to forget in a middle-of-the-night gab with that not-so-sly fox."

"Is this some sort of experiment? You're in on it too? Because I feel like they're drugging me here, making me see things and hear things."

"From the corridor you're in, I'd guess you feel this way because of a *lack* of drugs, a contrast to your former existence. This is a good opportunity to get clean for your babies. St. Kell's detox program is excellent, it's funded by the Assembly. If you're here it's because a transfer will be in order in a few months' time. It's lovely down there in the nursery wing. I don't know how long you can stay. I mean eventually it becomes a conundrum of imprisoning the children, doesn't it? But your case will be revisited several times. Let's not get ahead of ourselves now."

"I really think they're giving me something; I can't think clearly. I just feel so strange, so heavy."

"Maybe you're finally making peace with gravity. Or, like I said, you're in this corridor for a reason. My staff are good. They can see the addiction that haunts people across lifetimes, in your case across continents. Is that an American accent that you're wearing?"

"Yes, I…I came her a year ago. I didn't mean to stay so long. I was working there, at the Assembly. I've served you coffee before, Sir. And I was once the person who handed a pen to the person who hands you pens."

"Marten," he says with the kind smile. "And I know. He told me about you. Someone finally killed that bastard, Nicky. I'm grateful, actually. He willed the land to me that you'll be moving to next. Until he died, the prison nursery was in limbo." He pauses and continues, "Anyway, pay attention to what Aunt Vicky tells you. I haven't come across her in some time. Pay attention without trying too hard. You need to make yourself remember what she says."

"You mean what he says. The chaplain is a man, Sir."

Nils Winter rises to leave as Marten returns with word of a strategic photo opportunity down the corridor. "Just listen. Aunt Vicky's words may be the only truth you'll ever know." Laney's eyes follow the warden out the barred gate and nods her heavy head.

Over the next week, Maître Topoglu comes every second day, but the chaplain takes his time to return. Laney wonders if it's because she's finally sleeping again, and no longer getting trapped in the interstices between states of consciousness. Nausea now wakes her and heat pushes her out of her cot each morning. Her stomach has a firm spot where the twins are pushing against the outside, but not yet big enough for anyone to notice.

By the time her system is cleaned out and pregnancy hormones have taken over, she's been appointed mopping duty in the hallway above hers. It looks identical, down to the details in the peeling paint, and she lingers at the cell just above hers. He's in there. The chaplain is sitting in the cell as if it's perfectly normal to have switched sides of the grate. "Aunt Vicky," she says, her smelly mop quivering in hand.

I hear you've been looking for me, he says with a grin. He stands and pushes two metal bars apart to step into the hallway. No, he's not leaving, he's inviting her in. Before realizing what she's doing, the bars are back in place, inflexible and peeling like the walls. It's happened so quickly, before the mop has had a chance to fall to ground. They both watch through the bars as it clacks to the floor. Vicky is on the other side now, back in her cell, but a level up and close enough to the chaplain to smell the turmeric he's been cooking with.

Laney, what do you think is down below?

"It's me, I'm down below, in my cell. Or maybe I'm here, I don't know. I don't know anything anymore. My children will be born in prison, to a murderer. Isn't that all that matters anymore? Does it really matter which floor I'm on?"

Laney, I'm not talking about one floor down. All the way down, under the prison. What's there, Laney? Are you there? Holding someone?

Laney looks down at her hands, but now they're twisting around the braided, knotty mop. The mop head is somehow drier, cleaner than moments before. It's the Quipu. This isn't another cell, it's the chaplain's office. Does the chaplain have an office? Laney looks from one angle and sees an exact replica of her cell, but she can also see the chaplain's furniture, the painting of Lady Europe and something else. Two bodies, their fingers laced together in strobing blue light. She sees herself and Nicky. No, his name is Nico. But he's the same. Standing over the pair are Warden Winter and someone else. Who is he?

152

Aunt Vicky echoes the question from her mind.

Who is he? Do you recognize him?

"Should I? Is he my father?"

No, not in the way you're imagining anyway, no. He's older, a bit chubbier, but look at his eyes, Laney. Who is he? Who is the man from Argentina?

"It's Nico. But…how is he Nico? How can he be both people?"

He been goin' down the longest rabbit hole with you, child. Dropped you right in so gravity could suck you down with him. The chaplain's speech is changing with every word.

"Obviously, I don't understand, Aunt Vicky. I don't understand a thing."

You weren't made to understand, darlin'. You's a tool. A sacrifice. But you got some ideas of your own. I don't know how, but you do. See, Nico, he's Marka Swandish. He's Mo. He's me. He's even you. A thousand times back.

"Who's Marka? Mo? I don't – I don't…"

Yes, you do. You know all of them folks. And they know you. But, they all came from somewhere else, from Nico. Far as I can tell, Nico read an article about an inmate who used to be an intern at the Assembly, a scientist on the bioethics panel. Sound familiar? The article didn't give name, but Nico was drawn in because she was imprisoned in the town his family was from, way back, before he was born. This scientist, whoever she was, was tryin' to block a project on human brain simulation, worked with Andrei Soltanovsky, Carl Enders, all them usual suspects. They knew about the project at St. Kell and tried to block it. Legally, at first. They took it to the European Court of Human Rights, but aint nobody understood. Their case was thrown out and the rest of them got some desk jobs and the equivalent of tape over their mouths, but the woman ended up in jail. Maybe that was part of the plan. Went on hunger strike, that woman, until her big, beautiful ball of hair started to wilt. She lost her hair, probably lost her mind. But she got closer to the Vicki. Became an addict in there, exchangin' tators with the neighbor boy over the prison wall. Started sendin' messages in those potatoes too. Messages about what needed to be done. Where to go, what to do. How to slay the bull. Well, the kid on the other side of the wall found the Vicki, but he didn't destroy it. Not even close. He wrote about it online and Nico read it with wide eyes. The kid figured out how to turn the machine on, Sugar, just like you did. And he published that woman's story just before he tripped the switch. Or at least that's how Nico understood it. Everybody I make interprets things in such funny ways.

"Everyone you make?"

It's too much for your simulated brain, child, too much to comprehend. But I be makin' all of this. I be curious too. My machine's a bit different though, doesn't work the same way. But it creates. Makes things out of other things.

"What things?"

Raw materials. The things I know from the world I came from, the one I was made in. You can't make a sculpture out of somethin' you don't know. You make it out of clay. Or stone. Marble. Not nothin'. You can't make somethin' out of nothin', child. I made a simulation out of what I knew. Marka, that's the woman in the prison, and she' be the closest thing I know to being me. She's an extension of me, a better me, I guess. See, the problem with runnin' a simulation usin' what you know is that you create a sim that will do the same. Nico turned that thing on. Made God knows how many different strings of possibilities.

"God knows? Do you know?"

I lost count, Sugar, but you can consider it infinite. And I'm sure each one's got a bunch of curious characters lookin' to do the same, thinkin' they're revolutionary.

"So I don't have four cones in my eyes? Whoever told me that anyway?"

Laney, you don't even have eyes. That's the beauty of it, Sugar. Objects aint got color, they just bounce light back and your eyes interpret it that way. Color don't exist and somehow, you made more of it. Nico just loved that. And he just adores you, even though you's part of him. He thinks he's too creative to be cuttin' *beef in Queens so he spends his days thinkin' you up. Thinkin' of anythin' just so he don't concentrate too hard and slice his hand off as he makes the same cut all day, carcass after carcass. That's what this is. All you've ever known is a fraction of a daydream in the mind of a bored butcher who might-a had a family in France, way back when.*

You think you's the one tryin' to carry him through to whatever is next, but you got it all backwards. In one of trillions of strings, he came up with you and he can't let you go, fold you back in. Maybe he met someone, learned somethin', who knows? But he got an idea of you and he wants to keep you just like you want to keep him. So what you turned on, he's tryin' to destroy. He aint got memory of where he came from, just like you don't when you're in those lives, those strings. All you know is that you have to keep following your track, pushin' on just like a beam of light.

He done tried thousands of tweaks to get you right. But you needed to be darker, so dark and empty that you's a vessel, a black hole. Somethin' that can absorb ideas, suck them in. You had to have a sister, a twin, and give her all your light to make you that vessel. But with that emptiness, all you can do is look back, wonder what might-a been. Wonder what was missin' for you so you can get it back.

"But I don't want anything back. I still don't even know what was missing."

It doesn't matter, child. It just matters that you are who you are for this short time. This split second that's been divided umpteen times. Nico's done it in this string, he's made it come to an end. That car is about to blow, Laney, and you will go with it. You, Nico, the Vicki and those other two underground dreamers who think they're alive.

"But what do you mean by Carl being Nico? I still don't understand how they can both be Nico."

You's built to recognize patterns, Laney. Look and you'll see the underlyin' structure. Look at the bones in all those different faces. They all be different skins stretched over the same truth. Nico's inserted himself from another simulation, only earlier, so he could meet your dad. Make a difference earlier on. It took him awhile to perfect, but he needed you to be Carl's daughter, the real Carl's daughter. He needed Carl to make the Vicki. Nico wasn't inspired alone. So he came as an Argentinian, which is pretty silly if you ask me. He aint got any knowledge of South America. That's all just because St. Kell or Strasbourg, wherever that kid came from was called Argentina a thousand years ago. The Argentoratum.

"In real life? Or in the simulation?"

Laney, I don't know if there is, or ever was, a real life. Everythin' I know could be part of somethin' else. My version of the Vicki allows me to see into my creations, like I'm doin' now. I like to give guidance, when it's needed. I like to answer prayers, Laney. But I don't know if anyone be listenin' to mine. What I do know is that you have a choice here, but you need to make it very soon. These strings of life are slidin' by in colors and tones, heavin' through the ether around you, but you need to look for 'em to see. Grab hold-a one now. You's still underground, child, holdin' that boy's hand. If you think you can find a way to keep him, you'd better do it soon or you'll be buried.

'What do you mean, buried?"

Aint nothing below Strasbourg. Nothin' underground. The Cathedral's practically floatin' on water, held up by wooden beams plunged into a wet mess. St. Kell's built on a flood plain, child. Try to dig down to find some truth, all you'll get is wet. That's just one of the infinite things that a daydreamer in Queens wouldn't know.

"Aunt Vicky—" She starts and stops at the same instant. She's in her cell. Hot, sweaty and alone. The wet sheet tells her she's been here all along. A sing-song voice of a chaplain fades into the daylight streaming through the bars.

ARC-EN-CIEL

Nico walks next to her, in proximity as if they were holding hands, but both know this is not acceptable so they keep a cushion of air between themselves. Every day after school he brings her around Saint Kell, but every trip takes a different path. Yesterday, they'd visited the goats that live upstream on an island in the middle of the Argent River. The day before, they'd thrown old chunks of baguette to the ducks and swans. But her favorite walk with her student had been when he took her over a bridge, across the river, to a sparkling lake, *la gravière*, in the middle of the Ostwald forest. They'd momentarily gotten lost in the woods, which now seems to have been orchestrated by Nico. The forest is quite small.

Today he is bringing her to a tunnel that connects two pieces of path and runs under a railroad line.

"I painted this tunnel when I was in *collège*," he says.

"You weren't in college, Nico. It's called middle school or junior high."

They enjoy correcting each other's false cognates, what Nico calls *faux amis* or "false friends," itself an example of the group of words that sound similar in French and English, but have different meanings entirely. It had started when Laney first came to dinner at Nico's and told his grandmother that French apricot jam had far fewer condoms in it than the American version, which had made Mamama laugh so hard, her gold teeth had almost fallen out.

Their dialogue is a constant dance between French and English, each borrowing words from the other in a seamless banter that doesn't make sense to most people around them. Laney cannot tell anymore whether she is speaking Nico's language or he is speaking hers, only that they are communicating like no one she's met before. It's dizzying and worrisome, but she needs to get more.

"So you painted this tunnel? A giant mouth, Nico?" She takes in the toothy façade at the entry to the tunnel, wanting to take apart its symbolism, but coming up blank.

"Well, Mo designed it, actually. He said he was inspired by my mouth though. When I was a kid, I had too many teeth and they had to pull some out." *A kid*, like he wasn't still one now. Laney pictures the artist Mo, another boy in her English class. At 17, they're both almost adults, but also her students, and the thought makes her feel sick as Nico continues. "But see, if you walk through, you can see the other side. That's the side I wanted to paint. Our whole class worked on it at Hans Arp, but Mo and I did most of the heavy lifting. We wanted it to be perfect."

"What's Hans Arp?"

"That was our *collège*...sorry...our middle school. It was named after an artist who was trying to figure out the universe."

Laney smiles as she looks at the naïveté of Nico, knowing that all artists are trying to figure out the universe, that he was probably doing the same as he painted the tunnel. That every street in this part of St. Kell was named for dead men who had wandered around their worlds with paintbrushes, trying to make some sense of it. She is giddy to see Nico's brushstrokes, impatient to see the other side. But he stops her in the middle of the tunnel. The sun must be directly overhead because the light shines in from both sides, but leaves a patch of dark in the center for the teacher and student. He's looking at her intently, but not speaking. All she wants in this moment is to feel his wild thoughts swirl around in hers.

"I'm trying to figure out you, Nico. Tell me something I don't know about you."

"There are a million things you don't know about me, Laney. You'd have to live a million lives to know me well."

"Then you're a complex kid. Well, if you tell me one thing, it's a start. In other worlds, I'll learn something different about you. Maybe I'll put it all together and know a million details. My mom taught me that there are countless universes that we can't see. Membranes slapping together to create life and experience."

"I'd like to slap my membranes on yours, Laney."

"That's the worst line anyone has ever used to flirt with me, young man."

"That's not flirting. *Flirt* in French is something else."

"What do you mean, Nico? Another of your *faux amis*?"

"Not really, it's almost the same, but more like this." He covers her mouth with his and transfers an inordinate amount of passion for a schoolboy. Laney can't stop herself from kissing him back, not realizing her hand has reached the back of his neck, pulling him even closer. She holds him there in the dark too long. She's falling too fast and a wave of dread works its way through her body as she pulls back and looks at the boy's face.

"No, Nico. Not like this. In another life, I promise."

Nico takes a step back and is suddenly nonchalant, something adolescents pull off so well. "So are you coming for dinner tonight? Mamama's cooking." Laney's dread turns to anxious guilt as she realizes she's come too close, that she's to blame for this unsuitable relationship, and that she's come to dinner at the Arbogasts too many times.

"I can't, Nico. I can't...but I will." She grabs his hand in hers for a few brief seconds, still hidden by the shadows, then squeezes and lets go. "Come on, show me the other side."

They step into the sun and turn around to view the other entrance to the tunnel, and everything has changed again. Nico is just her tour guide, and they're on a platonic visit of the neighborhood. The tunnel is decorated like a rainbow. It looks freshly painted and pristine, almost new, like the pillowcases Marka Swandish gave the twins as welcome home presents after the adoption. Redorangeyellowgreenbluepurple. "I love it," she says to Nico, but she means it as another love, one she can't speak. The rainbow is so simplified, so delineated and two-dimensional. So easy to understand.

Nico's eyes are shining. They're beautiful eyes, dark but warm. Had she noticed them before? She can feel his will to keep the tears from spilling over. "Thanks," he says. "I thought you would. So, tell me about your mom. What's this membrane slapping all about?" She still doesn't know what language they're speaking.

"She studies brane cosmology. It treats our existence as a series sheets moving around, like they're on 2 clotheslines and the wind is blowing them together."

"So your universe is made of laundry?"

"No, the universe is the contact, the moment that two surfaces come together and draw back apart. That's where we are, in one of infinite collisions of branes. But other people think there's no such thing as matter at all, just tiny curled up strings, gyrating and vibrating in little loops. They're all just trying to understand what we're in, what we're part of. Like your old school's artist, I guess. Mr. Arp. My mom really believes in her work. When she'd bring us to Nigeria to see the family, they all thought she was a bit nuts. My grandparents in Lagos are super Christian and they say her work is dangerous. I think that's why she came to the States. That way she could do her work without everyone looking over her shoulder."

"Nigeria, Laney? I don't get it. You don't look like you eat bush meat."

"That should offend me, Nico. Not everyone in Nigeria eats bush meat. I do, by the way, and it's delicious. But that's beside the point. Anyway, I'm adopted. My dad died when I was four, from a brain infection. He worked with my mom and she adopted us. My family is my mom and my sister. And our extended family is in Nigeria. What about you, Nico? What's your story? I've met Mamama, but why aren't your parents ever around? You never even talk about them."

"Well maybe love skips a generation for them, I don't know. They didn't have any problem moving to New York and having Mamama raise us. They left France to grow grapes. They left the best white wine region in the world to go grow grapes in New York, go figure. They come back three times a year with lots of presents, but it's kind of bullshit. They've been there for a few years now, since we lost the house and moved to the apartment."

"Wow. I can't imagine my mom doing that. But then again, she left her family behind, in a way. And I guess coming here, I've left her behind too, although it's only for a school year. But my mom would never leave me or my sister. She gave up her whole life for us."

160

"What do you mean? She must have been so happy to raise you. To be your mom. She's lucky, Laney. She didn't give anything up."

"She was happy. She is happy. She tells us all the time. But she was really getting ahead in her field back when the accident happened with my dad. He was nuts and got this infection after drilling a hole in his skull. It was his own fault, but my mom still feels like it was hers, like she led him on in some way. Well, they had worked on all these way-out-there type of projects on light and color. She said they even tested some of their theories on Vicky and me because we had special eyes. They'd have us ride around in a fake hot air balloon and measure all this crazy stuff. I don't recall most of it, but she showed me some of the pictures."

"What's with the special eyes, Laney?"

"My sister and I are tetrachromats. It's not very interesting, really. Even goldfish have four cones and they're not revolutionizing the universe, but I guess it made us different from most people. I can't tell that I'm any different, but apparently I can see more colors than you can because of the extra cones in our eyes. That's not why I love your rainbow, by the way, just because it looks different to me. I'd love it even if were all grey, Nico." She pauses to see his reaction. She's said too much again and has to keep talking to erase the awkwardness.

"How does it look to you though? Does it look different?"

"I don't know Nico, I can't see it like you do. But, no, I think because it's painted I can see it as you intended it. A real rainbow in the sky though, that's hard for me to look at. There aren't wide arcs like you drew, like you painted. There are thousands of pinstripes, so many that they almost aren't there. Like I said, it's hard to look at. Even harder to describe.

"Anyway, when my dad died, my mom didn't want to experiment on us and knew she wouldn't be able to help herself, so she changed fields. She lost her funding. Had to start all over. She did that for us. She's always been concerned about being equal with us, with my sister and me. The first time I really knew that she was my mom was only two days after my dad died. We had a vacation bible school concert and she insisted we go, even though we hadn't unpacked yet, even though she said we didn't 'match,' that our hair was black, but different textures and people would look at us in funny ways. She said we had to get back on a routine, back to normal life. After the concert, she lifted us both up in a hug us and said, 'I could pick both of your pretty voices out of that whole choir, my little goldfish. Your wavelengths each entered a separate ear.' We were so happy to have her there, clapping her hands along to our ten variations of 'Jesus Loves Me.' I don't think our first mother ever came to those things, at least I don't remember if she did. I don't really remember her at all, I can't see her face. Just the sight of her walking out of the pizza place and never coming back. I don't think she planned on me seeing her leave. Our dad even had a social worker come over and tell us she was dead, that she drowned or something. But I saw her leave. I never told anyone that, so consider yourself lucky."

"I consider myself lucky just to talk to you," says Nico as his shoulder brushes up against hers. She feels a shiver that she shouldn't feel.

"It's nice to have someone to talk to here, Nico, but you know this could seem inappropriate to most people. I'm supposed to be a mentor, an employee, not a friend."

"How about a little friend? *Une petite amie?*" he said, grinning.

"I know what that means, Nico. In English, they call that a girlfriend and it's out of the question. You're a child."

"I'm not a child. I've had lots of *petites amies* already, Laney. It's not a big deal." This statement has the unfortunate effect of making Laney feel both jealous and perturbed that her heart thumps for a near juvenile. She is twenty-five after all, and had never contemplated falling for a student when she took this job. She fears and craves the things she imagines happening in the shadows of the rainbow tunnel. If only they had met later.

"I need some space, Nico. I think I need to cancel for dinner tonight. Tell Mamama *bonjour* and that I will actually try her rabbit sometime."

"You know she was just joking, Laney. She hasn't cooked rabbit since the move. She'd only cooked the ones she raised and there's no room in an apartment for bunnies. But I will tell her you said hi. She likes you. *Moi, je t'aime bien aussi.*" Laney is stuck with the sticky task of deciphering the French "I love you so much too," knowing that the *bien* actually weakens the statement to a casual "like." Part of her hates the word "bien."

"I'll see you tomorrow, Nico, after school. Where are we going, anyway?"

"Do you want to go to the lake in the woods?"

"But we've already been there Nico, I thought you were the tour guide.

Always something new."

"Yes, but I know you liked it there. If you really like a place, if you feel good there, what's wrong with going back to it?" His words carry more weight than usual, like he's speaking across dimensions.

"Okay, then, see you tomorrow. Meet at the school and then we'll cross the bridge together."

*

They've walked up the incline over the rainbow bridge to the train tracks and Laney takes in the vista around her. Long grasses show the pattern of the wind and she wants to stay here forever, to walk around talking to Nico for all time. Every day she pours out a bit more of herself for discussion.

"Nature or nurture, we're all carrying a burden of the past. My mom knows just about everything. Or at least a little about everything. She's a jack of all scientific disciplines. She told me that epigenetics marks people, that it's possible to feel our ancestors' pain. That generations of men and women who worked in Austrian salt mines are written on my DNA from my birth mother's side. She says my mitochondria know what it feels like to be buried in salt. I don't know if I believe her, by the way."

"I don't feel a burden, I never have. I don't know how some people carry so much weight with them. Look here, where the train goes. My brother, Val, is working for the SNCF. He's going to be a conductor for the Paris-Strasbourg route. It pays well, but they say statistically every conductor will come across a suicide at least once during their career. Someone so burdened to just lay down on the tracks."

"Are you kidding? There are that many?"

"Yes, and the worst part is that the conductors can see them from really far away. Sometimes they're even standing up, but the train has too much momentum. They can't stop something as heavy as a train in its tracks. Not in time anyway. So they're told to just blow the horn and close their eyes."

"Nico, if I hadn't left the US, I would have married someone who wears baggy khaki pants and prepares corporate tax returns. I guess that's my train."

"So you found a way to avoid the disaster. You had to derail."

"Maybe I saved the guy on the tracks, but killed everyone on board by changing course. Maybe, no matter what I do, it's wrong. Because what I want is *you*, and you're all wrong, Nico." She's said it. *I want you.* And saying it only makes it seem more wrong than before.

He takes her with a grip that means things will happen and there's burning, blood pumping into every capillary, every spot left neglected too long. Pulsing that makes her face pink as Nico starts to pull so many parts of her down.

His kisses are not refined by age and he's too wet, too eager. But she pulls him closer still, like she's pulling life itself into her. He meets no resistance as he slides in and out, nestled in sharp weeds by the train tracks.

They both know the sound of the evening train, a sound that means they've walked too long, that it's either dinner or scandal and they must move on. But both lie nearly motionless, just a fraction of Nico shrinking, but still inside Laney in the bushes as they breathe each other in. A tear that seems too hot is rolling down Laney's cheek. She cannot keep this moment. He kisses her again, almost like a man this time, with a long, slow, even pressure normally taught by time.

"*Je t'aime*," he says, so simply that it could be comedy, without adding a *bien* or a *beaucoup*. A full-scale I love you from what amounts to a teenage boy. Before she can protest or threaten a move back over the Atlantic, his mouth is secured around her left nipple and pulling it up in a 'pop' that shivers her core. His fingers have worked their way down and inside her, replacing his sticky appendage with powerful fingers. Laney is picturing the dirt of his hands riding up inside her and it only makes her glow warmer. Rough and rhythmic, it can't be lasting but a minute, but she begs for more time and looks at his face. His beautiful face, marked with experience by a long scar, but more handsome than anything she's seen. His eyes are on her, in her through his fingertips as she sees what she thinks must be some form of understanding.

Then, before she can tell him he's changed her, that he's shaken her to the core, he's re-pantsing and hopping on one foot, trying to get dressed before going to the evening meal in his tower block. He is so clearly seventeen. Laney stands and brushes grass off herself, feeling the textured imprint of broad weeds on her derrière. It takes her a moment to realize she's fully naked in the late summer sunlight at dinnertime.

Nico has applied one shoe and is looking for the other before the train crosses to block their path for four minutes or more. "Here it is," he says proudly as Laney's insides still pulse with longing for the boy who is already on his way home. They can see the train now and the time has more than come for Laney to clothe herself. Nico stumbles, inebriated onto the tracks as his nature-clad lover looks on with melancholy.

The train is too close now. Shouldn't he be moving? Why is he still standing there? Then she sees. Sees the bright white laces of his shoes, stuck on something in the tracks. He's tugging, working at the knot. Why doesn't he just take off the shoe? But the more he pulls, the tighter it gets and he's still tugging as the horn starts blowing, a sound so heavy it pushes Laney back. She's standing there, half hidden in the bushes, naked and panicked with nipples that could not be more erect as she looks to the conductor. He has placed his arms in an X in front of his face so that he cannot see what transpires before him.

BALLERINO

Consider the thick ballerina. Her legs are two Iberian hams, stretched perfectly straight, but not forming a line as a featherweight should. The strong, firm bulges have the disadvantage of causing each tap of the toe to become an artful thump. It is clear to all but the dancer that she is a tutu-clad textbook case of excess androgens. She knows as she draws her acned face to the warmth of the spotlight that this will be her final performance as the rest of the troupe takes to the road without her. Theirs will be a world of playing pocket-sized girlfriends and hearing voices quiver at the power of their stickly silhouettes.

She only hopes that she, too, has a face in the dark of the auditorium, one that is quickly becoming charmed into obsession over her unconventional frame. But she knows with a persistent ache deep between her shoulder blades that she could only be the recipient of deferred appreciation, like a home with vinyl siding. Disgust would give way to beauty for her spectator, coming full circle as it tended to do, but she would need millions more minutes than the two in the spotlight could afford. The classical piano notes tinkle to a halt and she's meant to quickly bend a delicate knee in goodbye, then flit off stage with a name too common to trace and footsteps to light to follow.

Not so long down the road, the ballerina's middle begins to pour into the sink as she brushes her teeth, leaving a bar of dried toothpaste on her control top garments, just below her waistline. And soon, like the last birds of summer, her waistline has disappeared. She is left alone in front of the mirror, staring back at the chin behind her chin, the greater stealing the focus from the lesser. Her shoulders curve in arcs down to her padded wrists.

Pizza calls her from the kitchen, singing a love song she knows from another lifetime. She can feel the savory-sour-softness of the marinara on her tongue, stretch the mozzarella and squish its rubbery saltiness in her teeth. Copious doses of olive oil and fresh basil slide down her throat. Quantity begins to win out on quality and it's now a personal challenge to see how much will stay down. When thoroughly compressed, the pizza sends out its grips from the fridge, not yet abandoned long enough to grow cold. One more slice will fit. But she is wrong. Three more fit with some tamping down. The seasons change and so does her body. The iron core remains, but becomes enveloped by expanding cells she cannot recognize.

Her legs rub together as she walks. Then everything starts to rub. Such a chafing, heaving object she's become. She eats until she can no more. But still the butter calls. The biscuit crust. The pesto sauce. Smoked Gouda. It's a dream brought into daylight, but it's never good enough.

And then come the dark days. She can no longer rise from her bed, no longer fit into a car to be dually weighed and scorned by that smug Indian doctor. All that had once been firm is buried alive in pulsing folds. Two home health aides unsuccessfully hide their disgust by her bedpan and her smell. But one day a sub comes by.

He has a ribbed black turtleneck and stands on his tiptoes to reach over her shame, wiping the creases under her folds. He speaks no English, but points to himself and says, "Nicolas."

She lays awake all night begging whatever gods may be to send Nicolas back. An answer comes through an azure grin at the foot of her bed, then dissipates before hitting her ears.

You can't take him with you, he'll only meet a thousand ends.

The agency has keys. After all, she's upstairs, up the curving staircase fit for a more lithe southern belle. She hears the front door open and light footsteps climb the stairs and approach her room. He's come back. And he's smiling.

He comes back over and over again. Quiet and calm. He prepares her pizza, then holds it up for her to see. To her surprise, he cuts it in half. Then he sits down next to her at a small table he must have found by the door downstairs and proceeds to eat his half with a knife and fork.

A week later, Nicolas is bringing wine and salad to eat along with their pizza. And after one month, he looks at her without speaking, putting his hands out and lifting them up in a biblical motion that bellows, "Rise!"

She giggles and feels her chin ripple. Is it pulling away from her neck just a bit? She grasps the bed frame that has imprisoned her and pushes off. She's standing now, like she hasn't stood in months. Once step forward feels like dancing and Nicolas turns in a tight circle with a toe touching a knee. His arms go out, then in, a perfect arc ending in two fingertips hovering together. Nicolas has the balance of a someone who's been dressed at one point as a swan or a nutcracker.

He brings music now and throws his toes straight up in glorious leaps across the bedroom. He takes her hand and twirls her heavy body until it becomes light again, if only for a moment. She's ready now, ready to leave with him. She's lost enough of herself to make it out the bedroom door. He walks her, no dances her, over to the curved stairs. She knows now the only thing to do is an artful arabesque before beginning her life below.

She lifts her leaden leg and throws her arms to grace. But her other leg must now hold the whole project and it fails its hopeless task. A wobble becomes a tumble and before she can tell what direction she's dipped, she's rolling, snowballing Nicolas and dragging him down the stairs. For two-and-one-fourth seconds, they're dancing, twirling around as they go down. In a flash of finality, she looks down to her outstretched thighs at the bottom of the stairwell where she's crushed her nurse in a hasty death.

ENCIERRO

Nikola_Tesla_1984: Thanks for joining private room
  Laneybird1: You going to kill me now or show me your weiner lol?
Nikola_Tesla_1984: My camera is covered with electrical tape!
Nikola_Tesla_1984: Otherwise I might ;) but not a murderer btw.
Nikola_Tesla_1984: So you got my attention. Is it true?
  Laneybird1: Yep, George Viereck was my grampa.
  Laneybird1: R U a skinhead or something?
Nikola_Tesla_1984: ??
  Laneybird1: Grampa had a wall-sized Nazi flag in his basement
  Laneybird1: and named his dog Rommel
Nikola_Tesla_1984: he was Nikola Tesla's best friend, that's why I care.
Nikola_Tesla_1984: Nazi = douche either way though
Nikola_Tesla_1984: What do u remember about him?
  Laneybird1: Green pumpkin seeds
  Laneybird1: And his dog
  Laneybird1: The dog wasn't a nazi lol
  Laneybird1: His grandfather was Kaiser Wilhelm
  Laneybird1: My grampa's granpa, not the dog's
Nikola_Tesla_1984: You're shitting me
  Laneybird1: I shit thee not. I'm a descendant of Queen Victoria
  Laneybird1: So what's the deal with Tesla? And my gramps?
  Laneybird1: What's your real name
Nikola_Tesla_1984: Nick
  Laneybird1: Do you read Orwell or are you just a baby?
Nikola_Tesla_1984: Both :) but yes, born in 84. You?
  Laneybird1: Laney and I'm too old for you!
Nikola_Tesla_1984: Age is just a number
  Laneybird1: An important #

Nikola_Tesla_1984: disagree

Laneybird1: Agree to disagree?

Nikola_Tesla_1984: Agreed R U really in Queens too?

Laneybird1: Live in Minnesota, but I'm here for 5 days. You?

Nikola_Tesla_1984: Near Ithaca, Finger Lakes.

Nikola_Tesla_1984: But I'm living with my sister in the city

Nikola_Tesla_1984: until I can find a new job.

Laneybird1: Finger Lakes? Ur from there?

Nikola_Tesla_1984: My brother Val has a winery.

Nikola_Tesla_1984: Our parents are from Alsace and moved us here

Nikola_Tesla_1984: as kids. Val wanted to bring Alsace with.

Nikola_Tesla_1984: He makes Riesling.

Laneybird1: Yum

Nikola_Tesla_1984: Indeed. Want a bottle? :)

Laneybird1: Yes

Laneybird1: Maybe 2 !!

Nikola_Tesla_1984: The oldest wine in the world is underground

Nikola_Tesla_1984: in Strasbourg where my Mamama lives.

Nikola_Tesla_1984: I'll take you sometime?

Laneybird1: I wish! How old is it?

Nikola_Tesla_1984: Checking Wikipedia

Nikola_Tesla_1984: 1472

Laneybird1: That is old! Vinegar?

Nikola_Tesla_1984: Mamama says she tried it, but probably not true!

Nikola_Tesla_1984: Only presidents get a taste

Laneybird1: So really, why Tesla? Why u interesterested in my

Laneybird1: dead family members?

Laneybird1: Sorry for typing

Nikola_Tesla_1984: What you said in the main room about Ceres

Nikola_Tesla_1984: about the salt

Laneybird1: ?

Laneybird1: R U still there?

Nikola_Tesla_1984: yes, had to pee

Laneybird1: Ew

Nikola_Tesla_1984: You don't pee?

Laneybird1: Whatev. It is salt though. On Ceres

Laneybird1: Don't you think? What else could it be?

Nikola_Tesla_1984: They say the spots are the size of Las Vegas.

Nikola_Tesla_1984: Just sayin

Laneybird1: That's ridic. Salt, Nick

Laneybird1: Salt!

Nikola_Tesla_1984: Did you really work on the launch of Dawn?

Nikola_Tesla_1984: Or was that to lure me into a private room?

Laneybird1: I thought you were doing the luring
Nikola_Tesla_1984: Oh yeah, yur right
Nikola_Tesla_1984: but what did you do for Dawn?
Laneybird1: I was an accountant
Nikola_Tesla_1984: yawn no really
Laneybird1: Really. I did get project updates though.
Laneybird1: I was sort of in the loop
Nikola_Tesla_1984: Loopy
Laneybird1: Loop-de-loop
Laneybird1: U RA dork
Nikola_Tesla_1984 :I know, that's why you love me.
Laneybird1: You move fast, kiddo
Nikola_Tesla_1984: Older women in science turn me on
Laneybird1: Even accountants?
Nikola_Tesla_1984: of course
Laneybird1: Why does everyone in that room believe
Laneybird1: Ceres is something else?> More than salt?
Laneybird1: On a dwarf planet?
Nikola_Tesla_1984: Well, it is intriguing.
Nikola_Tesla_1984: The sports are so bright.
Laneybird1: sports?
Nikola_Tesla_1984: SPOTS
Nikola_Tesla_1984: Maybe it should mean something
Laneybird1: Maybe you just want it mean something
Laneybird1: We'll find out in August next year
Laneybird1: When Dawn flies closer
Laneybird1: Been waiting since the launch in 07 for images
Nikola_Tesla_1984: want to watch together?
Laneybird1: Lol it's not a show. Probably a silent time elapse video
Laneybird1: on you tube
Nikola_Tesla_1984: groovy
Nikola_Tesla_1984: So I'll bring popcorn?
Laneybird1: Seriously, tell me about yourself
Nikola_Tesla_1984: So I'm Nick. I'm 31.
Laneybird1: Already told me that!
Nikola_Tesla_1984: It was in case you can't do math. What about you?
Laneybird1: I'm 39. Grey eyes, black hair. Short.
Nikola_Tesla_1984: You or your hair?
Laneybird1: Both. You?
Nikola_Tesla_1984: I'm not a giant either. 5'9"
Laneybird1: You beat me. :) 5'4"
Nikola_Tesla_1984: So what else?
Laneybird1: I live for pizza. Hate drinking milk

Nikola_Tesla_1984: so no mustache?

Nikola_Tesla_1984: what else?

Laneybird1:I don't like drinking coffee from navy blue mugs

Nikola_Tesla_1984: You must get that from grandpa's side

Nikola_Tesla_1984:You know, white supremacy

Laneybird1: Har de har har

Nikola_Tesla_1984: K, what else? Family?

Laneybird1: I have a twin sister

Nikola_Tesla_1984: Is she hot?

Laneybird1: i hope so, We're identical

Nikola_Tesla_1984: :)

Laneybird1: My dad's from Mexico and don't have a mom,

Laneybird1: but she's the side you're interested in.

Laneybird1: Her dad was Tesla's buddy

Nikola_Tesla_1984: No mom, but have a mom?

Laneybird1: She left, not just us, but everyone. Left the nazi too.

Laneybird1: I don't know her, but knew her dad.

Laneybird1: He made good pancakes. My own dad married a dude.

Nikola_Tesla_1984: So two dads?

Laneybird1: 2's better than one! One's my step dad.

Laneybird1: They live in Mexico though.

Nikola_Tesla_1984: Do you visit?

Laneybird1: They come here. I've never left the country.

Nikola_Tesla_1984: Really? Maybe I'll take you somewhere :)

Laneybird1: To France? That's where Alsace is right?

Nikola_Tesla_1984: Oui! I've been there twice, but it's hard

Nikola_Tesla_1984: if you don't speak German.

Laneybird1: French?

Laneybird1: You mean French

Nikola_Tesla_1984: In Paris, in Strasbourg, yes. But my relatives are in a

Nikola_Tesla_1984: weird village and they only speak Alsatian.

Nikola_Tesla_1984: It's kind of like Swiss German I guess.

Laneybird1: Ok

Nikola_Tesla_1984: I also went on an art school trip to Paris

Laneybird1:Groan

Laneybird1: Of course you went to art school

Nikola_Tesla_1984:I ended up dropping out.

Nikola_Tesla_1984: The trip to paris was the best part of the program

Laneybird1: I think you have to be a dropout to be a real artist lol!

Laneybird1: So did you see anything life-changing as a blooming

Laneybird1: artist?

Nikola_Tesla_1984: Giverny, Cluny, Rodin, Louvre

Laneybird1: Did the Mona Lisa look at you?

Nikola_Tesla_1984: Just smiled. She's littler than you'd think.

Laneybird1: What's Cluny? George's gallery :) ?

Nikola_Tesla_1984: They have la Dame à la licorne

Nikola_Tesla_1984:Lady and the unicorn. It's mideivel

Nikola_Tesla_1984: Medieval (had to spellcheck that one) tapestries.

Nikola_Tesla_1984:They're tapestries of the 5 senses, but what's cool is

Nikola_Tesla_1984: all that's going on around the subjects. they don't

Nikola_Tesla_1984: seem to notice everything in the air around them.

Laneybird1:Sounds trippy

Nikola_Tesla_1984: Yep. I loved it

Nikola_Tesla_1984: U'd probably like Rodin though.

Laneybird1:And how do u know?

Nikola_Tesla_1984: Cuz you're female! His museum is a house

Nikola_Tesla_1984: with a garden. Lovers come right out of rocks

Nikola_Tesla_1984: there, they come into being together, entwined.

Laneybird1: This is me blushing!

Laneybird1: sculptures are so eerie to me. They capture a moment,

Laneybird1: but they could also capture a moment that hasn't been.

Nikola_Tesla_1984: Well, life inspires art, but art inspires life

Nikola_Tesla_1984:or so they say

Laneybird1:THat's imagination, right? Art influences life?

Laneybird1: Maybe the artist creating it makes it true somehow.

Nikola_Tesla_1984: That's what I thought, but then I saw this little

Nikola_Tesla_1984: old woman. at Rodin. It was so raw, so painful to

Nikola_Tesla_1984: look at her. She couldn't have been more than a

Nikola_Tesla_1984: foot high.

Nikola_Tesla_1984 :La misere, it was calledt. Miss Misery.

Laneybird1: Ok, i assume you're talking about a sculpture,

Laneybird1: not a real lady?

Nikola_Tesla_1984: That's the thing! All I could do was hope she was

Nikola_Tesla_1984: imagined, that she wasn't real. But how could the

Nikola_Tesla_1984: detail be there? She was bent over so u could see

Nikola_Tesla_1984: th pain Even her spine was sad.

Laneybird1:   :(

Nikola_Tesla_1984: But how could he make her so real?

Nikola_Tesla_1984: he had to know someone suffering that much.

Nikola_Tesla_1984: And if he really imagined it, then wasn't he

Nikola_Tesla_1984: creating suffering by putting her into being?

Nikola_Tesla_1984: ?

Nikola_Tesla_1984: Sorry, I'm crreeping you out

Laneybird1: no, just thinking…

Laneybird1: Maybe the statue suffered so she didn't have to.

Laneybird1: So the idea of her could be there without the misery.

Laneybird1: Maybe Rodin's a kind of savior :)
Nikola_Tesla_1984: maybe! but It wasn't even Rodin, I guess it was
Nikola_Tesla_1984: a friend of his who made it.
Laneybird1: So we're agreed that you're taking me to Paris then?
Nikola_Tesla_1984: How about we start small. Queens.
Nikola_Tesla_1984: Or a bit beyond. I can take you to Wardenclyffe
Laneybird1:??
Nikola_Tesla_1984: On Long Island. It's where Tesla built his tower.
Laneybird1:??
Nikola_Tesla_1984: Wardenclyffe Tower = free energy for all
Nikola_Tesla_1984: I'm sure you can see why it didn't work!
Laneybird1: So it's still there?
Nikola_Tesla_1984: Tower = No, But the energy is. Want to come?
Laneybird1: Are you nuts?
Nikola_Tesla_1984: Yes, let's go on a field trip.
Nikola_Tesla_1984: Something better to do?
Nikola_Tesla_1984: So?
Nikola_Tesla_1984: Want to come?
Laneybird1: Actually I do!
Nikola_Tesla_1984: Really? Or???
Laneybird1: Really. Or let's talk anyway.
Laneybird1: I think i need to talk 2 you. 612-293-5803
Nikola_Tesla_1984: I'll call u

Nikola_Tesla_1984: That was weird Laney
Laneybird1: I know
Nikola_Tesla_1984: I could hear you smiling
Laneybird1: Still smiling.
Nikola_Tesla_1984: :)
Laneybird1: I've never told anyone that befor
Nikola_Tesla_1984: I'll take it to my grave.
Laneybird1: Not anytime soon please, we haven't met yet!
Nikola_Tesla_1984: So do you want to?
Laneybird1: Y
Nikola_Tesla_1984: I feel like I know you
Laneybird1: Me too
Nikola_Tesla_1984: Really know you though. It's weird.
Nikola_Tesla_1984: Are you hungry? I know a good noodle place.
Nikola_Tesla_1984:?
Nikola_Tesla_1984:?
Nikola_Tesla_1984: Still there?
Laneybird1: Still here. I do know you, Nick. I don't know how,

Laneybird1: but I know you. I think I've been looking for you.
Nikola_Tesla_1984: :)
    Laneybird1: There's a huge Hindu temple across the street from me.
    Laneybird1: I can see it through my window.
    Laneybird1: Think about it
    Laneybird1: There's even a statue there! A guy with tons of arms
    Laneybird1: and crazy hair. Right outside my window
Nikola_Tesla_1984: If it's a Hindu temple, that's Shiva.
Nikola_Tesla_1984: I hear he's a good dancer
Nikola_Tesla_1984: so think we're reincarnated or something?
Nikola_Tesla_1984: my aunt used to call me an old soul
Nikola_Tesla_1984: Someone who's already died a thousand deaths.
Nikola_Tesla_1984: think we met in another life?
    Laneybird1: I don't know
    Laneybird1: Nick
    Laneybird1: Just will be glad to meet you
Nikola_Tesla_1984: so noodles?
    Laneybird1: Nooldes!
    Laneybird1: Sorry
    Laneybird1: Noodles!
Nikola_Tesla_1984: Lamian Ping in an hour?
    Laneybird1: Checking where that is from here
    Laneybird1: 45 minutes
Nikola_Tesla_1984: oK
    Laneybird1: You didn't tell me what u look like
    Laneybird1: You didn't tell me what you look like
    Laneybird1: Did you leave yet?
Nikola_Tesla_1984: Laney
Nikola_Tesla_1984: Remember, You'll know me

Laney has the address for Lamian Ping. It's only a 20 minute walk from the Hindu temple, a building with an out-of-place ornateness in Flushing, Queens. A disheveled man is ripping open a package of tube socks on the sidewalk in front of the temple. "Cheaper than laundry, Sugar," he says as Laney steps past him. There's something about he pronounces the last word "shoe-ga" with such musicality that it makes her turn around and look into the man's jaundiced eyes. She feels a pang of regret as he sends her a yellow wink and proceeds to change his socks.

The restaurant is in a sprawling food court below street level and Laney takes an escalator into a teeming chatter that smells like everything she's ever inhaled all at once. She scans the signs, but can't read the black characters.

拉 面 平

Under the sign is a beautiful woman with dark hair so long that it reaches below the cuffs of her white shorts. She's pulling and twisting and punching a blob of dough on a metal counter. Her nametag says Nancy.

Nancy's thin arms spread straight out like wings and Laney can see the dough become strings. Her hands work quickly and the movements can't be isolated, but suddenly there are four ropes, then eight. Nancy steps away from the counter and folds the noodles into a steaming pot. As she separates from the counter, Laney notices her lower half. Nancy's short white shorts reveal two long, thin legs, one of flesh and one of carved wood. Laney makes no effort not to stare as her eyes trace the viny, floral pattern wood-burned into the leg from the cuff of her shorts down to her delicate wooden ankle tucked into a canvas shoe. The leg is meant to be a thing of beauty more than function, but Nancy moves with more grace than expected from behind the counter to where Laney is standing. She picks up a menu with the same coded characters as the room around her and motions to a Formica table with two chairs.

"I'm waiting for someone," says Laney, but she can tell by the woman's non-reaction that she doesn't understand. Nancy stays next to the table and places the menu that must have been laminated years prior into Laney's hands. She can't decipher the characters and the pictures are nearly hidden behind the film of a thousand fingerprints. "I'll just...thank you." But Nancy stays, waiting for a command Laney can't possibly give.

She wants to wait for Nick. To see if he looks how she imagines and to ask if he, too, will skip the beef today. Nick will know what to order here, must know what to say. But for now, all the greyed-over bowls on the page look the same. She wants more than anything for Nancy to go back to her post so she can watch the mesmerizing noodles again as she waits for her date to come down the escalator. But Nancy grabs her hand and a spark travels up her arm as she moves Laney's finger down the page. She stops at an indiscernible bowl and looks to Laney for agreement. Laney sees the outline of a hand-drawn carrot, the nearly ubiquitous symbol for a vegetarian dish, and squeezes Nancy's hand to confirm. The pressure of the clasp is returned by the waitress, a silent *I am here*.

Nancy is still hovering over Laney when a shout comes from behind the counter. "Ping!" followed by a string of mounting and descending words in quick succession by a mustachioed superior wearing a dirty apron. Nancy gives a quick grin and releases her hand, then turns back to the open kitchen. Laney feels her eyes travel along the groove in her leg, twisting and bending along the wood-burned motif, wishing she could run her fingers along the tendrils and feel their texture. Soon Nancy is back to pounding and stretching, twisting the dough until it folds in on itself. But as she pulls her arms back out, Laney see the separate strings again and she can't take her eyes off the culinary display.

She doesn't know how much times has passed. She has slurped through the solid contents of the savory soup by battling with chopsticks decorated in patterns that quite resemble Nancy's leg. She looks left and right before bringing the bowl to her lips to sip the umami concerto that lingers on the bottom. Accepting that her luck in a chat room was too good to be true, that she would only lead her faceless lover through another thousand deaths, Laney pays at the counter and concedes that Nick is not coming. She nods in Nancy's direction and rides the escalator back to the surface.

She has to leave New York in less than a week and return to the autumn leaves of Minnesota. Fragments of plans she's already started sketching swirl around her head, plans that now seem too Nick-heavy to be reasonable. Laney finds herself walking, knowing not where she's headed as long as it's nowhere she's been. She walks for what must be half an hour to a vast park, willing the disappointment out of her body with each step forward. The red-green of the trees seems to breathe her in and exhale her onto a paved clearing. Up and overhead is a tired metal globe, surrounded by fountains; she's seen this somewhere before. It must be from the World's Fair. Flushing, 1965. Her grandfather would have been here. Maybe Nick would have come for him. The metal on the globe no longer gleams, but still holds the hopes and dreams of decades past within its matte-grey sphere.

Surrounding the fountain is a temporary exhibition of sculptures, a group of stationary figures that seem discordant in their variety. It seems fitting to end up here after the morning's otherworldly exchange. Laney has almost made a full circle and stops at the last statue. Someone has left a paper coffee cup at the base, with its steamy contents curling up to the metal above it. It's a statue of a gigantesque woman with a perfect metal ball of hair coming out the back of her head. She wears a long coat and her face is smooth and kind. She's holding someone up, someone smaller, an old woman crumpled in pain. Even cast in unyielding metal it looks like the large woman is in motion, infinitely catching the other from free-fall and holding her tight. Laney senses the suspended potential energy of the woman dropping to the floor as she studies the sculpture. A commotion off to her right turns her head.

Two men burst from the trees, chasing after something black. Somehow the scene is happening too fast and Laney can't place what's going on. There's a bull with ruffled fur that makes it looks like a stuffed animal found in a consignment shop. The animal's labored, swinging gait shows that the chase has been long. It likely started with an exhilarating liberation, but three tranquilizer darts prove the end is near for the bovine.

The bull's hooves are not accustomed to the concrete of Queens and are a constant reminder that the animal is far from home. It collapses in front of the globe and one of the men runs over, laughing. "He wanted to see the Unisphere!" he says and walks toward the heaving animal. A small crowd has gathered. "Thanks for your help, man. I'm sorry that took longer than expected. And this is the third one to escape this year! I'm telling the boss we need a better gate." He walks over to the other man, now panting like the bull as he recovers from an unplanned chase and offers his hand. "You'd better get to that appointment, buddy."

The men shake hands and the sweatier of the two walks over to the bull, noticing Laney as she looks on, horrified. "This happens more than you might think, Miss."

Laney asks if the bull is going back to the slaughterhouse.

"A sanctuary will probably take him. Look, he got out, right? We're not bringing him back. He just needs to go somewhere else. Can't have a bull wandering around the streets of Queens." His face is a bit squinty and his head drips with sweat, but he's handsome. So much so that she has difficulty meeting his eyes. When she finally does, her heart pounds ferociously, threatening to crack her ribs. She sees something dark and fast rising up behind the man, but she can't look away from his dark regard. The bull is standing, pushing, trampling. The man's body is shoved against the base of the statue and a dark spot appears on his shirt where a horn or hoof must have gone through. His eyes lock back to Laney's as his chest now makes small quick movements up and down. He opens his mouth as his body lay leaking, trying to speak, but no words come out as a hot tear slips out of Laney's eye. Instead the air is speaking directly to her, a whisper carried by the coming winter to pronounce two words from beyond the realm of anything she knows. She looks to the dying man and smiles.

"You were right. I do know you, Nick."

GUESH URVA
(2011)

Notes began to fall into place in a cave beneath a prison, wavelengths so clear as to form a picture, one that could not be ambiguous in showing Nico his error. His hands were tangled up in Laney's, like branches of olive trees growing too close. But also there was Mithras in his freedom cap, his knee on the beast, a dagger plunged into a region void of vital arteries. He was looking over his shoulder, looking at the sun god who had commanded the sacrifice. He was pulling the bull's head up by the nostrils, trying to calm him and thus capturing the moment before a revolution. The plot twist of Mithras' sacrifice was being immortalized in stone. He'd done as instructed, but in preparation for reprisal, when he'd push with his knee to pull the dagger out and face his commander. He'd placed the knife just so, avoiding a deadly placement of the jab. Mithras, keeper of livestock, was not slaying the bull. He was saving it.

The weight of understanding kept Nico's eyelids shut, his body immobilized as he realized the gravity of his prior interpretation of the tauroctony. As thousands of lifetimes rode by in a technicolor stream, babies kicked, mounds were built, dreams were crushed on stairs and Shiva kept dancing through Nico's ever-inevitable death. Nils and Carlos perceived only a mere second in the passage of time, but Vicky and Nico's faces were suddenly stained with experience. A weary line stretched between each pair of brows and a tear slid down Vicky's cheek as she mourned Nico's untimely ends. The lights flickered as a smoldering Mercedes Knight on the other side of the wall prepared to ignite with the beat of a drum. Nils reached down to grab the pair of enlaced hands and brought his lips to Vicky's ear, then whispered a timeless two-word command, one that would echo through even red-green trees of a park in Queens.

"Go forward."

PISCINE À BALLES

The twins are doing somersaults off the edge of the ball pit when it starts. They're enjoying making a baby giggle as he sits in the lap of a golden-toothed woman who calls him Nicolas. She's dangling her legs in the balls like they're water and bouncing the smiling boy. Later, Laney will sit on her mom's knees next to the same woman at the support group. She will be holding her grandson and trying to forget the face of the *lunatique*, the gunman too easily influenced by the pull of the moon.

The man charges in and fires more shots than the children yet know how to count, pointing his weapon this way and that, aligned with his oddly serene stare. By the time he aims at the tiny boy, Vicky is already flying through the air in a jubilant flip, blissfully unaware that she'll intercept the bit of hot metal and won't come down the same. It is the last time Laney sees her sister's face, so much her own, but reflected more brightly back. An open casket will be out of the question due to the placement of the hole, punched by a bullet just through the center of her forehead in a neat little circle. Her father, pizza in hand across the room, remarks immediately that the pressure in his own head has abated.

The noises are so loud that they cease to be separate, mixing into a single transparent note and holding a confident hum. The life has left her sister, but Laney still holds her hand through the whir as she looks up to see her mother. Time has slowed until near silence now; she can see every chaotic motion of Claire's about-face as she turns away from the shaft of light. She's dropped her purse, filled with burdens of individual ambition, and she's pushing through the ether. Running, running back.

CITATIONS

The following works swirled around Nico's head, begging for a place in life's conversations:

Coleridge, Samuel Taylor. Rime of the Ancient Mariner. New York: Appleton & Co., 1857.

Shakespeare, William. Sonnets 14 & 71